THE OLYMPIANS

PART ONE

RYAN A. HERRING

120
pages

First Printing, 2017

ISBN-10: 1-947197-02-9
ISBN-13: 978-1-947197-02-2

120pages
Subway Sites LLC
PO BOX 231548
New York, NY 10023

120pages.com

HOW TO READ A SCREENPLAY

A screenplay is written to show, not tell. They are written to convey how a film would unfold. The writing is crafted to evoke vivid images without describing them directly, but by carefully setting a scene that unfolds in a telling or revealing way through the words and actions of the characters. As such, words are used economically. There is less description than you would find in a novel, as those details are typically handled during the production process.

Therefore, as you read, visualize a film in your mind and "see" it as if you were watching a film.

If you're not familiar with the screenplay format, here are some things to know:

SCENE HEADINGS
Scene headings describe where the action is taking place, the time of day, and some other important details, such as if it is a flashback, a montage, etc.

For example:

```
INT. SAMMY'S HOUSE - DAY
```

"INT" indicates the action is indoors. "SAMMY'S HOUSE" tells us the action is in a woman's house. "DAY" tells us that it is daytime.

```
EXT. PARK - NIGHT
```

"EXT" indicates the action is outdoors. "PARK" tells us we are in a park. "NIGHT" tells us that it is the evening.

Other time descriptions may be used, such as "SAME" to indicate action taking place simultaneously or "LATER" to indicate action taking moments later, after a brief jump in time.

CAPITALIZED WORDS
Throughout a screenplay, you may come across CAPITALIZED WORDS. These generally indicate the introduction of a new character, that the camera should pay attention to a particular item/sound/person/location, or that we are moving into a specific place within the location.

For example:

```
John turns.  He sees SALLY, the most beautiful girl he has ever
laid eyes on.  In her hands, she holds AN ADORABLE PUPPY.
```

DIALOGUE
Dialogue is written by centering a character's name. Their spoken words appear beneath their name. For example:

```
                    JOHN
          You found Charlie!
```

PARANTHETICALS

Between the character's name and dialogue, you may see text in parenthesis. This indicates some specific direction about how the dialogue is to be read or some specific action that takes place in the delivery of the dialogue.

```
                        JOHN
                  (eyes watering)
            You found Charlie!
```

OTHER TERMS

Some other terms you may need to know:

(O.S.)or (O.C.) – Off-screen or off-camera indicates that we do not see a character when dialogue is heard

(V.O.) – indicates voiceover. This is dialogue we hear, but the speaker is not physically present in the same location as the action

(CONT'D) – Indicates that the same character is continuing to deliver a line of dialogue after an action, scene change, or other note is written.

(MORE) – Indicates that the dialogue from the character continues on the next page.

POV – Indicates that we see the action through a defined point of view

SUPERIMPOSE – indicates that we see text on screen, typically to define a time or location

MONTAGE – indicates rapid cutting of different scenes in a sequence. For example, any training sequence in a Rocky movie.

(beat) – indicates that a character takes a brief pause before continuing dialogue

I would like to dedicate this book to my beautiful and supporting wife, Molly, who always gives me the encouragement and advice I need to keep going.

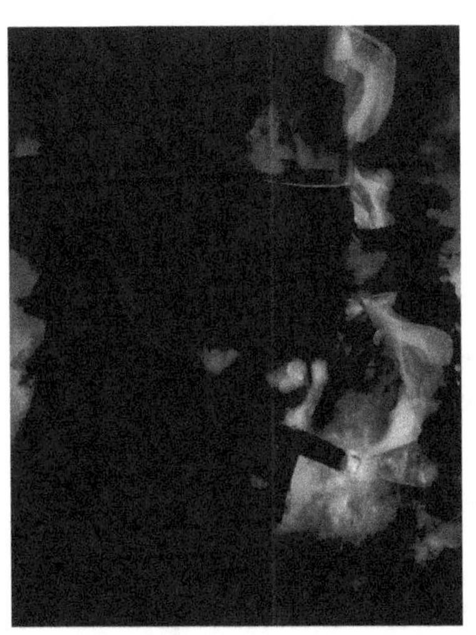

EXT. CALIFORNIA DESERT - SUNRISE

ON-SREEN TEXT: "1871 Gilroy, California"

Seven men ride on horseback with the brilliant morning sun
rising behind them. They appear as a black silhouette against
the large golden disc that shimmers above the desert floor.

Dust billows behind them in a flowing cloud as they race
across the horizon.

They wear long duster jackets and are all heavily armed.

The man in front wears a star-shaped metal badge pinned to
his dusty jacket. It catches the morning sun and flashes as
he rises and falls in the fast rhythm of his running horse.

The badge reads "Sheriff."

They approach a ravine and slow to a trot. They ride along
the edge of the ravine for a short distance.

The SHERIFF motions for them to stop. They dismount and sneak
silently to the edge of the ravine.

From behind the posse, we see them looking down at a small
cabin. The Sheriff motions to them and they quietly move down
the ravine in a single-file line.

They sneak up close to the small, dilapidated cabin on foot.

The Sheriff motions and the men spread out and surround the
cabin.

Everyone gets into position. They stir restlessly. They all
look at the Sheriff, waiting.

The Sheriff looks back at his men, then at the cabin. He
takes a cigar from a pocket in his jacket and lights it with
a match.

He looks back at the two men just behind him. He motions to
one, a younger man.

                        SHERIFF
              Jacob. Get up here, boy.

JACOB hesitates nervously for a second, then steps up and
kneels beside the Sheriff.

On his jacket he has a badge that reads "Deputy."

2.

                         SHERIFF
               Time to earn that badge, son. Sneak
               up close and see how many we got.
               Word is they had quite a little
               celebration after the heist they
               pulled yesterday, so if we're
               lucky, they're still sleeping it
               off. Remember, look for Ingram and
               Poole. If we can get both of them
               two, the rest of these vermin
               should scatter.

Jacob looks at the other men, all safely hidden. He sees
several cruel smiles looking back.

                         JACOB
               You want me to go in alone? What if
               they got alarms set and I walk into
               an ambush?

                         SHERIFF
               Well, you best pay attention and
               try not to get yourself killed,
               then.

The Sheriff grunts and spits a brown slimy glob at Jacob's
feet. Jacob hears several quiet snickers.

He tightens his jaw and pulls out his pistol. He starts to
creep forward slowly.

                         JACOB
                    (under his breath)
               Thanks, Dad.

Jacob sneaks up slowly toward the back door of the cabin. He
keeps low and moves in against a wall.

Slowly, he walks beneath a window.

He cautiously looks in. Men are strewn about, still sleeping
off what looks to be a very rowdy night.

He ducks back down and looks toward his father and the
others. The ends of several rifles can be seen poking out
from behind various cover.

He smiles to himself, then starts back briskly.

As he passes the outhouse, he steps up beside it briefly,
pressing against the side, looking around cautiously.

He takes a step forward.

As he does, a knife slips around his throat, and he hears -
CLICK!

- the hammer of a pistol being cocked. He feels hot, rancid
breath on his neck.

                    RUFUS INGRAM
          Hold it right there, sweetheart.
          We're going for a little ride, you,
          me, and all my men. Now you give me
          that pistol, boy.

RUFUS, 38, takes the pistol from Jacob and tucks it into his
belt.

He presses his gun hard into Jacob's back.

                    RUFUS INGRAM
          Now, you tell that sheriff of yours
          we ain't going to no jail cells.
          Not today. If he's got any interest
          in seeing you alive, he best take
          his posse back up the canyon and
          let us ride out of here. When we
          hit the Mexican border, we'll set
          you free.

                    JACOB
          Tell him yourself.

CRACK!

Rufus smacks Jacob in the back of the head with his gun.

Jacob crumples to the ground in agony.

                    RUFUS INGRAM
          Don't play tough, boy. It don't
          suit you. Now, stand up so they can
          see you whimper.

Rufus grabs Jacob and pulls him to his feet.

He prods him forward out where everyone can see clearly.

                    RUFUS INGRAM
          Sheriff John Hicks Adams. I have
          your deputy. If you want the boy
          back alive, take your posse back up
          the canyon and let me and my men
          ride out of here free. I give you
          my word we'll let the boy go after
          we hit the Mexican border.

4.

There is commotion in the cabin. The men are rousing quickly
and readying for battle.

Glass breaks out of windows and rifles stick out of the
jagged holes.

Jacob scans the posse for any sign of movement.

Silence. Then --

BOOM!

With a violent explosion of blood, a bullet tears through
Jacob's shoulder and hits Rufus in the chest.

Rufus stumbles back. Blood burbles out of a ragged hole in
his chest. He gargles and spits blood.

A second round tears out his throat and he falls dead in a
spreading pool of blood, steaming in the cool morning air.

Jacob falls to the ground. He looks at his ruined shoulder
with a bullet hole torn through it.

All at once, shots fill the air from both directions. Men
come pouring out of the cabin. The posse closes in, and the
air is filled with smoke and the screams of dying men.

INT. CABIN - NIGHT

Jacob sits on a table with his shirt off. A young woman,
HANNA, cleans his wounded shoulder. Jacob winces with pain.

                    HANNA
          Sorry, Jake. I know this stings.
          You poor thing. I can't believe he
          did this to you.

                    JACOB
          My pa is a man true to his word. He
          brought down the Ingram Gang just
          like he said he would. He wasn't
          gonna let me get in the way of his
          being the hero. The great sheriff
          Adams always gets his man.

Hanna begins to bandage the wound. Their eyes meet. They
share a moment, looking into each other's eyes.

Hanna touches Jacob's shoulder softly.

                    HANNA
          Your daddy's a hard man. That's
          what it takes to do what he does.
          But, that don't make it right,
          treating you the way he does.
          You're a good man, Jake.

                    JACOB
          Yeah, well, I'll never be the man
          my brother was. Not in pa's eyes.
          Since the day we got that damned
          letter, he never looked at me same.

Jacob pulls old an pocket watch, missing its chain, from his
pants pocket.

He opens to it reveal a photo on the inside the of cover. It
shows a handsome, young Union Soldier.

                    JACOB
          It's like, when he found out Johnny
          died... so did any kindness he had
          for me. Now, when I look in his
          eyes... all I see is burning
          hatred.

                    HANNA
          You're his son. He loves you. You
          just remind him of himself too
          much. And, for some reason, he
          hates that about you.

                    JACOB
          It's not him he sees when he looks
          at me. It's my ma. He used to tell
          me I reminded him of her. And I
          could see in his eyes that he loved
          me. But, that was before Mama died
          and Johnny went to war. Now...

He closes the watch and returns it to his pocket. He sighs
heavily.

                    JACOB
          ... I'll never be my own man until
          I'm free of his shadow. I'll never
          be a great lawman. I need to find
          my own path.

                    HANNA
          You are a great man, Jake, and you
          can be whatever you want to be.
          I'll always be here for you.

Hanna brushes Jacob's hair back gently and they lock eyes.

Slowly, they go in for a kiss.

Suddenly the Sheriff comes in, helped by another man. They hurry over and push Jacob aside.

The Sheriff sits on the table and the other man, BERT, 30, starts to take off the Sheriff's jacket.

> BERT
> Can't you see the Sheriff's been
> shot, woman? Help me, for God's
> sake.

Jacob grabs his shirt and jacket. He starts to dress himself painfully while Hanna takes over for Bert and removes the Sheriff's jacket, revealing a bloody tear in his vest on the right side.

> SHERIFF
> Easy, Bert. The bullet just grazed
> me is all. I ain't shot. I been
> shot enough times for real to know
> the difference.

He looks at Jacob.

> HANNA
> Well, let's take a look at what
> we've got here, Sheriff.

She gently opens his vest and lifts up his shirt.

There's a small scratch on his side behind a large bruise, already turning an angry shade of purple.

She replaces the vest where it was over the wound. She looks at the Sheriff for a moment, then reaches into the pocket of the vest.

She pulls out a silver pocket watch with a bullet-sized indent on the front and across one side.

> SHERIFF
> Well, I'll be damned. Would you
> look at that?

He grabs the watch and pulls up his shirt.

He places the watch where it would have been in the pocket, and the trail of the bullet is clearly seen.

                    BERT
          God damn, sir. You are one lucky
          dog. I gotta go and tell the boys.
          They ain't never gonna believe
          this.

Bert exits.

Jacob looks at the Sheriff for a moment, then notices him
staring back.

He turns and grabs his pistol belt and hat.

                    HANNA
          Well, it looks like that bullet
          broke a rib or two, so I'm gonna
          have to wrap it up for a few days.

She turns to get a bandage and Jacob turns to meet her gaze.

                    JACOB
          Thanks for patching me up, Hanna.

They stare into each others eyes for a moment, then Jacob
turns to leave.

Hanna turns and starts to bandage the Sheriff's side.

                    SHERIFF
               (to Jacob)
          You surprised me today, boy.

Jacob stops and turns his head slightly, but doesn't turn
around.

                    SHERIFF
          You didn't die.

Jacob walks off briskly and the Sheriff grins through the
pain of having his ribs bandaged.

INT. SHERIFF'S OFFICE - DAY

ON-SCREEN TEXT: "1873 Gilroy, California"

Jacob and another deputy relax in the office. Jacob stares
out of a small window at the distant ocean.

The other deputy cleans his rifle.

Jacob sees a large sailing ship, far in the distance, slowly
making its way across his window.

Closer, Jacob stares at the bay, which bustles with ships of all sizes.

Suddenly, the Sheriff bursts through the door.

> SHERIFF
> All right, boys, get your shit. We got 'em this time. I just got word that Mason and Henry and a few of their boys are shacked up in a cat house in San Jose. We're gonna ride up there tonight and give those bastards a little surprise. Now, get moving. We leave in twenty minutes.

The other deputy grabs his rifle, jacket, and hat. He exits.

Jacob continues to stares out the window, his mind seemingly elsewhere.

He feels the heat of his father's stare, and slowly turns to look at him.

> SHERIFF
> Why don't you sit this one out, boy? We need to move fast and I don't need to be dragging any dead weight. Unless you want to wake up and finally decide to be a man.

They stare at each other for a moment, then Jacob slowly lowers his gaze and turns to look back out the window.

> SHERIFF
> I didn't think so.

He grabs some shackles and a shotgun and exits.

Jacob stares for another moment at the sea, then turns angrily and grabs a shotgun and his jacket.

EXT. TOWN - SUNSET

The Sheriff leads a posse of nine men into a small town.

They approach a saloon and dismount.

The posse hitches up their horses and gather around the Sheriff.

                    SHERIFF
          Alright, listen up. Best we know,
          Mason, Henry, and five of his men
          are holed up somewhere in there.
          Now, what we got workin' for us is
          the element of surprise. So, once
          we get inside, you need to move
          fast and find your man.

He looks at Jacob.

                    SHERIFF
          I guess you made your decision, eh
          boy?

                    JACOB
          Maybe.

                    SHERIFF
          I hope so. You cover the back.
          Dewey, you stay out front. Shoot
          anything that comes through the
          door. Let's move.

Jacob heads around to the back of the saloon.

He stands in the shadow just behind the door.

After a moment -- BANG! BANG! -- gun shots, followed by
screams are heard from inside of the saloon.

Commotion.

Jacob looks around nervously.

He hears footsteps that seem to be swiftly approaching the
back door.

He softly creeps up the wall behind the door and presses
himself flat, waiting.

SLAM!

A man, HENRY JR, bursts out of the door.

Jacob steps out of the shadow and knocks him down with the
stock of his rifle.

He cocks both barrels and sticks it in the man's face.

                    JACOB
          Don't even think about moving or
          I'll blow your head clean off.

                    HENRY JR
          Shit! Whoa. Easy there, big man.
          Nobody wants to get anybody shot
          now, do we? I just wanna get out of
          this mess is all. Goddamn!

                    JACOB
          You just play it cool and do as I
          say, and you're not gonna get hurt.
          Now, let's just sit tight 'til the
          sheriff comes and takes care of
          you. You're gonna answer for what
          you done.

                    HENRY JR
          Well, see, that's just it. I ain't
          done nothing. I just rode out to
          meet the boys this morning. I
          didn't kill nobody. I swear...

Henry Jr studies Jacob for a moment.

                    HENRY JR
          You're the sheriff's son, ain't
          you?

                    JACOB
          So?

                    HENRY JR
          So, how's it feel to be the son of
          a famous lawman, and know that he's
          willing to shoot you down to get
          his man? Like he did with Rufus
          Ingram?

Jacob slams the barrel of his gun on Henry Jr's face.

                    JACOB
          Does that answer your question?

Henry Jr winces and spits blood. He holds up his hands
protectively.

                    HENRY JR
          Okay, okay, shit! Look, I know how
          you feel. I wouldn't be in this
          mess if it wasn't for my daddy and
          brothers. I don't want to die for
          their crimes. Look, I have what you
          need right here. I stole it from my
          brother Thomas. You take it. Here.

BANG! BANG!

There are several gunshots from inside. Sounds of running and
muffled yelling are be heard.

                    HENRY JR
          Take this loot I lifted from him
          too. Just, please, let me go.

Footsteps running closer, more shots.

He holds out a folded piece of paper and a small leather
purse that looks very full.

                    HENRY JR
          Please.

Jacob snatches up the purse and looks inside.

He looks back at Henry Jr and quickly pockets the purse.

Jacob snatches the paper and stares at it for a second.

WHAM!

The Sheriff and three other men burst out the door.

Jacob turns and slips the paper in his jacket pocket.

The Sheriff approaches, completely out of breath. He looks
around as he catches his breath. Henry Jr is gone.

                    SHERIFF
          Where's Henry Jr? We saw him come
          out this way. Weren't you watching
          the damn door, boy?

Jacob is silent. He looks down.

The Sheriff starts to yell at him, but he doesn't hear his
voice.

He sees the world in slow motion as his dad starts to beat
him violently.

EXT. STEAMSHIP - NIGHT

Jacob stands on the deck of a steam ship leaving San
Francisco Bay.

He looks down at a paper in his hand, the same one that Henry
Jr gave him.

He unfolds it.

12.

The paper reads: "FREE LAND! COME TO WASHINGTON TERRITORY!"

EXT. FOREST ROAD - MORNING

ON-SCREEN TEXT: "1874 Olympic Peninsula, Washington Territory
An endless sea of virgin old growth forests bordered by a
rugged Northwest Pacific coastline stretch out below majestic
snow capped mountains."

Jacob walks a horse down a narrow and muddy road running
through the thick forest of giant trees.

Jacob is dressed in a long duster jacket and armed with a
revolver hanging on his hip from a worn holster.

He also carries a double barrel shotgun in one hand. The
"Deputy" badge is gone.

He travels alone.

As he walks, he looks around nervously. His horse whinnies
and pulls on the bridle, coming to a sudden stop.

His arm is jerked and he grunts as he stumbles forward,
sliding in the thick mud. He turns back and pulls on the
bridle, clucking at his horse side-mouth to keep walking.

The horse whinnies again and snorts, shaking his head.

A sound beside him in the trees makes him turn. He raises
his shotgun quickly.

He looks around down his barrel.

Silence.

He sees a dark shape moving quickly through the trees.

His horse rears up in fright. Jacob quickly fires a shot!

BOOM!

Silence. The thick smoke from the shotgun slowly clears.
Nothing is there.

EXT. FOREST - NIGHT

Jacob sits beside a small fire in the woods, stirring a
steaming pot.

He takes a bite after blowing on it a couple times, then puts
the lid back on and returns the pot to the fire.

He pulls a cigar from a jacket pocket and pulls an ember from the fire. He lights the large, rough-looking cigar.

He sits back and puffs, looking around at the darkness surrounding him.

He pulls out paper and looks at it closely.

It is well worn, and he handles it carefully.

He studies it in the firelight.

The paper reads: "DISCOVER YOUR MANIFEST DESTINY! YOU NEED A FARM! COME TO WASHINGTON TERRITORY AND CLAIM YOUR PIECE OF PARADISE. THE HOMESTEAD ACT GUARANTEES EVERY MAN AND WOMAN FREE LAND OF RICH, FERTILE FARMLANDS TO COME AND MAKE THE LIFE OF YOUR DREAMS!"

He sits back and sighs, puffing on his cigar. Shakes his head in doubt.

Around him, from deep in the dark forest, strange noises echo like the call of some alien creature.

He grips his rifle tight on his lap.

                    JACOB
               (to self)
          What the hell am I doing?

EXT. FOREST - DAY

A thick rain forest. A Native American man, CHUKA, makes his way through the underbrush. He's not on a trail. He fights through thick under-growths of thorny brambles.

Chuka stops and leans on a tree, panting. He grabs a talisman on his neck hanging from a leather cord.

He closes his eyes and breathes deeply. He looks up through the trees and sees the mountains looming above.

He keeps going through the thick brush.

He crosses streams and struggles up rocky faces.

He falters a few times, but he continues on.

EXT. FOREST - NIGHT

Chuka huddles beneath the partial cover of a giant tree, shivering against the cold.

14.

The rain pounds his face. Wind whips through. We shakes
violently.

He clutches the talisman on his necklace and chants
repetitively.

His eyes are closed and he sways back and forth rhythmically.

                                        FLASHBACK TO:

EXT. NATIVE VILLAGE - DAY

Chuka is on beach in front of his village.

He mends a fishing net as he watches some men prepare to go
whaling.

An old man, SIYA, wearing a large bearskin wrapped around
him, approaches and watches the boy for a moment.

He steps up behind Chuka and puts a hand on his shoulder.
Chuka looks up and smiles.

MOMENTS LATER, they walk together in a forest. Sunlight
streaks through the tall trees.

                    SIYA
          When I was your age, my father told
          me to leave our home and journey to
          the heart of the river, deep in the
          mountain's roots. He said I was to
          go alone, take no food and no
          weapon to hunt or defend myself. He
          said, if the Great Spirits were
          pleased with me, they would reveal
          themselves. And they would give me
          power. I sent your father out on a
          journey with the same words, and he
          came back with great powers. Take
          this; it was his source of
          strength.

Siya holds out the talisman. Chuka slowly reaches out to grab
it.

                    SIYA
          Maybe it will guide you. Keep it
          close to your heart always. It is
          your time, my son. Go now into the
          mountain and see what the spirits
          have for you.

Chuka grabs the talisman and he hears Siya's voice echo out
in a haunting chant-like singing.

> SIYA
> I will be waiting. I will be
> waiting.

                                        BACK TO:

EXT. FOREST - NIGHT

Chuka continues to clasp the talisman.

The rain continues to whip his face. He shuts his eyes tight
and tightens his body into a ball.

EXT. ROAD - SUNSET

Jacob walks out of the thick woods and into a clearing on a
hill.

He stops and gazes at the water of the Straight of Jaun De
Fuca a few hundred yards below him.

Vancouver Island is a hazy shape in the distance across the
straight.

Below him, a small cluster of sailing ships are tied up to a
dock that juts out straight from the heavily wooded
shoreline.

Smoke curls up from a handful of buildings. Jacob tugs the
bridle and leads his horse toward the town.

EXT. PORT ANGELES - SUNSET

He walks out of the trees, off the muddy trail, and onto a
wider, but even muddier street running down to the waterfront
and the dock.

He passes several wooden shacks.

An old bearded man is standing in a doorway of a shack. The
old man stares at Jacob as he passes. Jacob nods and the old
man stares back.

Behind the old man, in the shack, Jacob sees several native
women staring back with blank expressions.

He passes another building that has a sign that reads
"Lauridsen Mercantile". Several large cows wander around in
front of it.

He pushes his way through, giving a large black cow a sharp
smack on the rear flank to clear it.

Jacob finds a large two-story building at the foot of a long
dock that runs out into the sea.

On a balcony above the entrance, several women in corsets and
lacy skirts watch Jacob as he hitches his horse.

Hanging off the balcony is a large banner that reads "The
Olympian House."

Jacob looks up at the women and tips his hat. They stare for
a moment, seeming to be shocked.

One of the girls cackles with hideous sounding laughter and
Jacob sees she is missing several teeth. The rest join in her
laughter as they watch Jacob flush.

Jacob grunts and walks inside.

INT. SALOON - NIGHT

Jacob enters and stands still. He surveys the room.

Several low wooden tables are strewn about with dirty, rough
looking men sitting at them. The men are drinking, smoking,
and playing cards.

A man plays on a violin plays in a dark corner. Several women
stand around a long, wooden bar. A few women sit among the
men, hanging on shoulders or sitting on laps.

The madame, a woman dressed in a fancy dress named FRANKIE,
stands behind the bar, next to a man in a white shirt and
black bow-tie.

Frankie is smoking a cigar and talking to a man standing at
the bar.

Everyone stops, turns, and looks at Jacob.

They turn away after a pause and return to their low
conversations.

Jacob walks up to the bar and looks at the bartender, but the
bartender looks away and pours another drink for the other
man.

Jacob smiles at Frankie. She ignores him, smiles at the other man, and they continue to talk.

The man says something quiet that Jacob can't hear and they both laugh and turn to look at Jacob.

Jacob quits smiling now and starts to tap impatiently on the bar with his finger.

Frankie ignores him and he becomes even more impatient. He sighs and clears his throat.

                    JACOB
          Madame, can I trouble you for a
          drink?

The Madame looks him up and down then says something quietly to the sailor at the other end of the bar.

They look at him, longer this time. Then they both laugh again. Jacob grits his teeth.

Another man, GUNDERSEN, a sailor, approaches the bar. Behind them, another man, BILL, watches them as he lights a pipe and puffs.

                    GUNDERSEN
          Where you from, bub? You ain't no
          seaman, and you're no whistle punk
          neither. So, what business you
          think you got here, dude?

                    JACOB
          I'm just a stranger, come into town
          and trying to get a quiet drink is
          all. You got a problem with that,
          sailor?

                    GUNDERSEN
          Maybe I do. So what are you gonna
          do about, dude?

Gundersen walks behind Jacob and leans in close to him. He sniffs. Gundersen smiles, revealing grey and black teeth.

                    GUNDERSEN
          This here bar's for working men,
          see. This ain't no place for a
          cocktail.

                    JACOB
          Look fella, I just got into town
          and all I wanna do is drink some
          whiskey in peace.

Gundersen glares at Jacob and slowly turns back to the bar.

Under his coat, Jacob's right hand slowly finds his pistol.

He slides it out and pulls back the hammer. It clicks.

CLICK!

Gundersen hears the hammer cock and pulls a huge revolver from his belt and points it at Jacob's back.

Suddenly, Bill steps in behind Gundersen and holds a knife to his throat.

                    BILL
          What's a matter now? Can't a
          stranger get a drink without having
          to smell your foul breath on him?

Gundersen grunts and Bill presses the knife harder. A trickle of blood emerges from where the knife presses into his throat.

Gundersen un-cocks the pistol and lowers his arm. Bill relaxes his hold and lets Gundersen slowly free himself, arms raised.

                    GUNDERSEN
          You fancy this city, boy? By all
          means, buy him a drink. I bet he
          smells sweeter than any o' these
          whores.

Gundersen jeers and cackles for a moment and then moves back to his group.

Jacob straightens up and returns his pistol to it's holster.

Bill walks up to the bar and grins, slamming his knife into the wooden bar top where it sticks, vibrating.

                    BILL
          Frankie, a bottle of whiskey for
          me... and my friend.

Frankie comes over and sets a bottle and two glasses down.

She stares at Jacob. Bill looks at Jacob and nods at the bottle.

                    JACOB
          Oh. Allow me.

He pulls out a couple coins and sets them on the bar.

Frankie snatches them up and shuffles off.

Bill picks up the bottle and pours the two glasses full.

He sets one down in front of Jacob. Bill plucks his knife from the bar and wipes it on his sleeve before putting it away.

He looks at Jacob and motions to a table off to the side.

Bill grabs the bottle and they pick up their glasses. They relocate to the small table.

Bill takes a big drink of whiskey.

                    BILL
          So stranger, what's your name?

                    JACOB
          Jacob Miller. Might I ask yours?

                    BILL
          Bill Hatch. Pleased to meet you,
          Mr. Miller. I wanted to tell you
          something, if you haven't already
          caught on. You know, you're only
          gonna get yourself killed dressed
          like you just stepped off the
          steamer from San Francisco, walking
          into a place like this.

                    JACOB
          Well, Mr. Hatch, the truth is I did
          just come from San Francisco. But
          I'm no dude. I'm no stranger to
          hard work.
               (drinks)
          Or a fight for that matter.

                    BILL
          Well, odds ain't so good on that
          one, Mr. Miller. This house stacks
          its hand heavy if you get my drift,
          and they don't exactly appreciate
          drifters or dandies. That lot
          wouldn't think twice about gutting
          you like a fish. And then, after
          taking any earthly possession they
          may find of value, the lovely
          Madame would have her girls drop
          your body off the pier. And no one
          here would blink an eye nor shed a
          tear.

                    JACOB
          I think I get the picture, Mr.
          Hatch.

                    BILL
          So what is it you're doing here,
          then, Mr. Miller? You don't seem
          like a business man exactly... more
          like a man searching for something.
          Or someone, maybe?

                    JACOB
          Like I said, right now I'm just
          looking for a quiet drink. For
          that, I thank you.

                    BILL
          So, what do you do, Mr. Miller?

                    JACOB
          Jacob. I was a deputy in a small
          town outside San Francisco, Santa
          Clara County. My pa was the
          Sheriff.
               (drinks, pause)
          Anyways, I gave up the life of a
          law man. I'm just looking to make
          an honest living. And maybe, if I'm
          lucky, find a place to call home.

                    BILL
          Well, you sure picked one hell of a
          place for that. This is a working
          man's paradise. Nothing but virgin
          old growth to be cut as far as you
          can see.

                    JACOB
          You a timberman, Mr. Hatch?

                    BILL
          Call me Bill, and yer looking at a
          third-generation logger. My
          grandfather was a logger in Ireland
          and England before he moved to
          Michigan. And the Hatch family's
          been logging its way west ever
          since.

A man, LOUIS BLAIR, bursts into the saloon, out of breath and
excited.

He goes up to the bar and slams his fist. The music stops and
men gather around.

                    BLAIR
          Dammit, Frankie, whiskey! Son of a
          bitch. We almost had him tonight,
          boys. Me and the hounds had him
          cornered and the devil slipped
          away.

Frankie walks up and pours him a glass.

                    FRANKIE
          So, did you see him this time, or
          did you just chase off after a
          shadow again?

                    BLAIR
          I saw him. With my own eyes.

                    FRANKIE
          Yeah? I hope so. Because no man
          comes and grandstands in my place
          unless he's got some earth-shaking
          news. Lest he be ready to buy the
          whole house the next round of pussy
          and drink.

Men laugh and grin and Blair looks around at the large crowd
nervously. He wipes his sweating brow.

                    BLAIR
          Frankie, you know I'd never mean
          you no disrespect. But, I seen him,
          God's honest truth I did. And I
          coulda' had that murderous beast
          too, if only my dogs were worth
          their flea-ragged hides.

                    FRANKIE
          Well then, trapper, tell us what
          the beast looked like.

She pours him a drink and slides the glass to him.

                    BLAIR
          Well, uh, he was moving fast,
          unnaturally fast. But, he was big!
          At least a head taller than a tall
          man. And he seemed to be covered
          all over in dark fur, except his
          face. That was the part that scared
          me more than anything. That face,
          it was like some demonic child.
          Grotesque, evil. My dogs had him
          cornered in a tangle up on Sawtooth
          Ridge.
                    (MORE)

                        BLAIR (CONT'D)
          But, when we got close, they
          wouldn't go in. I had to whip the
          piss outta my lead before she'd
          follow me. When we got there, he
          was gone.

Men huddle and talk excitedly around Blair as he continues
telling the story.

                        JACOB
               (to Bill)
          Who are they talking about?

                        BILL
          There's been some folks killed
          recently, homesteaders up in the
          foothills, and people say it was
          some sort of wild man that did it.
          Large footprints were found around
          the bodies and people say they've
          seen this large beast man running
          through the woods like a demon.
          There's even been talk of the
          federal Marshals coming in to hunt
          the beast.

Jacob smiles.

                        JACOB
          Wild killer beast man? That's a new
          one.

Bill raise his glass in a toast.

                        BILL
          Welcome to the Olympic peninsula.

EXT. FOREST - DAY

Chuka wanders beside a river.

He is delirious, and can barely hold himself up.

After staggering over some logs, he collapses on his face in
the sand.

As he lay there struggling to see, he has a vision of a fox,
who comes up and stands before him, seeming to wait for
something.

                        CHUKA
          What do you have for me, fox? I'm
          ready to receive my power.

The fox sits motionless, still.

Chuka tries to push himself up to his knees.

When he sits up, the fox is gone. He tries to clear his head and look around for the fox.

Suddenly, he spots the fox, fifty yards up the creek.

The fox turns suddenly and bounds into the underbrush.

                         CHUKA
               Hey, wait! Fox, wait.

He staggers to his feet and stumbles after the fox.

The fox leads him further up into the woods until finally it seems he lost him for good.

When he comes to the place where the fox was last standing, Chuka doesn't see the fox anywhere.

Dismayed and exhausted, Chuka slumps down against a tree in defeat.

He clutches the talisman and sobs.

                         CHUKA
               I'm sorry, father. I've let you
               down.

He holds the talisman up and looks at it.

                         CHUKA
               I'll never be great like you were.
               The spirits aren't with me. They
               aren't pleased by me.

He looks at the stone figure as it glistens in the sunlight, then lowers it. Above him, in the distance, he sees something behind where he was staring.

Suddenly he sits up and rubs his eyes.

High above him through the trees, he sees the fox sitting on a boulder.

It stands up and leaps off out of sight.

Chuka gets up and scrambles slowly up the boulder.

Behind the boulder lay steaming pools of sulfurs water laying in a rocky outcropping.

He stands in awe and then slowly wades into the larger pool.

> CHUKA
> The healing waters. They are real.
> The spirits have led me here.

He stretches out his arms and lets himself collapse into the water.

He lays under the water for a moment letting the steaming water flush his body and invigorate him.

He burst up out of the water as if born again and seeing the world for the first time.

His face is alight and he stretches his arms out and turns his face to the sky.

> CHUKA
> Thank you for this gift, Great
> Spirits. I will use these powers
> for the good of my people.

He grasps the talisman on his neck. He bows his head and closes his eyes.

> CHUKA
> Father, I will make you proud of
> me, you will see. I promise you.

EXT. FOREST - SUNSET

Jacob sits on a stump overlooking the Straight of Juan De Fuca, smoking a cigar.

He stands and pats his horse's head.

> JACOB
> What a ya think ole gal? Did we
> make a mistake leaving like we did?

The horse snorts and shakes its head. Jacob puffs and looks absently out at the setting sun melting into the water of the straight.

> JACOB
> I know, we just did what we had to.
> Come on, let's go get a drink.

INT. SALOON - NIGHT

Jacob sits at the bar, sipping a glass of whiskey.

TRACY, a prostitute who has been eyeing him, approaches and sits next to him.

                    TRACY
          What's your name, cowboy?

Jacob slowly takes another sip, then turns to Tracy.

                    JACOB
          Jacob.

                    TRACY
          Well, Jacob, you seem like a man
          who could use a tender touch.

She touches his hand softly.

He recoils after a slight pause.

                    JACOB
          Look, I'm just here for the
          whiskey, ma'am.

Tracy sets a hand on his shoulder.

                    TRACY
          Aw, c'mon Jake, don't be afraid.

Jacob grabs her hand tightly and squeezes.

                    JACOB
          Don't call me Jake. It's Jacob. Or
          Mr. Miller.

He throws her hand aside. Bill approaches from a dark corner.

                    TRACY
          Sor-rie fella, no need to get sour.

                    BILL
          Can't you see the man just want to
          drink in peace, Tracy? Now, piss
          off woman, until I'm ready for you.

Tracy stands and gives Jacob a seductive look.

Bill grabs her ass and gives it a good squeeze.

She slaps him hard, and he laughs heartily as she walks off.

                    BILL
          Devil minx. You made the right
          choice, passing up that one. She's
          as crafty as they come.
                    (MORE)

                    BILL (CONT'D)
          She'll take the clothes off your
          back if you fall asleep.

                    JACOB
          You don't seem to mind too much.

                    BILL
          Ha! I never fall asleep! Not in
          that spider's lair. A man does have
          his needs, Mr. Jacob. Truth be
          told, my preferred company resides
          at Port Crescent.

                    JACOB
          Port Crescent? Where's that?

                    BILL
          It's the glorified logging camp old
          man Lehman has out west of here,
          about twenty miles. Bastard is on
          his way to making it a real port
          town, complete with boardwalk,
          lodging, entertainment, even a damn
          general store. Rumor is he's trying
          to take over the county seat.

                    JACOB
          And he owns the logging outfit you
          work for?

                    BILL
          In Port Crescent, he owns
          everything. And everyone. But hell,
          the pay's good, and we have more
          trees to fell than I will see done
          in my lifetime. To me, this is
          heaven. The Olympics, Home of the
          Gods. Well, at least the biggest
          sticks I've ever cut. It can make a
          man feel almost small at times. But
          when your standing with your best
          boys and all o' you together can't
          reach your arm around the behemoth
          you just toppled, well it's kinda
          an indescribable feeling. It's what
          I live for.

                    JACOB
          Well I envy you, Mr. Hatch, that
          you've found the place you belong.

                    BILL
          Well, there's plenty o' work to be
          had for all that are man enough to
          do it. You should ride out to the
          camp with me in the morning. I'm
          sure we can find something to keep
          ya busy.

                    JACOB
          Thanks for the offer ,Bill. I'm not
          sure what I'll be doing next. I
          might see what opportunity there is
          for me here.

                    BILL
          Suit yourself, but you can always
          find me if you change your mind.

Bill eyes Tracy, who is waiting for him. Jacob smiles and
continues his drink.

MOMENTS LATER, Frankie approaches Jacob who now sits at a
table alone, playing cards and sipping a glass of whiskey.

                    FRANKIE
          A glass of limited reserve, from
          the boys. To show there's no hard
          feelings.

She motions to the sailors from the night before.

They grin hideous smiles and raise their glasses.

Jacob picks up the glass and nods. He sniffs cautiously.

He drinks. More drinks follow.

INT. SALOON, BEDROOM - NIGHT

Bill enters the room and closes the door, locking it behind
him.

He looks at Tracy with disgust, pity, and lust.

Tracy sits on her bed, with her back to the door and Bill.

She has a derringer in her hand and she's caressing it. She
is steaming with anger.

She waits a moment as Bill takes off his boots. Then, she
slips the derringer under her mattress and composes herself.

28.

As Bill approaches the bed, she stands suddenly and turns to
face him.

She slaps him across the face, hard.

Bill smiles and then delivers a vicious backhand to Tracy's
face.

Her mouth trickles blood. She starts to whimper.

Bill grabs Tracy by the shoulders and pushes her back to the
nearest wall and slams her against it.

                    BILL
          Have you gone mad, or do you wish
          to die tonight, you filthy whore?

                    TRACY
          I'm just trying to do my job is
          all. And you aim to interfere.

                    BILL
          What the devil do you mean, woman?
          I'm about to give you all the
          business you can handle.

                    TRACY
          That dude down there. You know I's
          making ready to lay my mark on him.
          And you come and get all bosomy
          with him. I'd a' thought Frankie
          had you working for her now too.

Bill digs his fingers into her shoulders and lifts her up
against the wall.

                    BILL
          Now, you listen, whore. And you let
          it sink in real nice. I don't give
          a rat's ass for Frankie or her
          damned pirates neither.

                    TRACY
          Well, I don't have that
          convenience. And now I'm gonna be
          in it with Frankie. I was supposed
          to help deliver six bodies for the
          morning tide. And now there's only
          five.

                    BILL
          Well, that's not anything to me you
          whimpering, fucking cunt.
                    (MORE)

                    BILL (CONT'D)
          And, if you ever so much as lay a
          finger on me in anger again, I'll
          cut that face of yours so bad not
          even a blind man will pay to fuck
          you.

Bill grabs Tracy by the throat and chokes her savagely.

Tracy gasps for air.

                    BILL
          'Sides, I'm sure Frankie has other
          means of securing her precious
          cargo, slippery fire crotch
          swindler that she is. She has her
          reputation to live up to, now
          doesn't she?

                    TRACY
               (whimpering)
          I'm sorry, Billy. Please... Let me
          make it up to you. Please...

Bill relaxes his grip slowly and lets her go.

He takes a step back.

She wipes her face off quickly then comes forward to kiss
him.

He slaps her again, hard.

Blood comes from her nose and she looks shocked.

He spins her around and presses her face into the wall.

                    BILL
          There won't be any of that. You
          should know better. You don't get
          to kiss me. Not there, darling.

He pulls out a knife and cuts her dress partly off.

He tears it the rest of the way off.

With his free hand he unbuckles his pants.

INT. SALOON - NIGHT

Jacob wakes to find himself laying on his face in the dirt.

It's dark except for a few torches.

His vision is blurry and he is confused.

He looks around and tries to move, but he can't get his limbs to move.

He groans and tries to speak, but his tongue is thick and stuck in his throat.

He opens his eyes again. Now, he sees a torch flickering and several shapes moving about him.

Then he hears voices.

> GUNDERSEN
> Start loading them into the dinghy.
> We need to get these stiffs ship-
> side before they start to wake.
> Captain'll have our necks stretched
> if we miss the morning tide. Start
> grabbing the shoulders, I'll grab
> the feet.

Jacob slips back into blackness.

Then he's dreaming... or in a drug induced flashback...

DISSOLVE TO:

INT. OPIUM DEN (FLASHBACK)

Blurry vision, eyes open slowly to reveal a dim and smokey room with oriental rugs and pillows lavishly strewn across low couches.

A large opium pipe sits smoking in the center of the room, and various characters are stretched out about the room.

An Asian man sits in front of the smoking pipe.

We look around the room slowly, through drugged eyes.

Then suddenly we hear a rising commotion outside, and voices talking loudly.

Suddenly the door bursts open and blinding light fills the room.

A large silhouette steps in through the light.

As he comes for us and grabs us by the shirt we see only the shiny reflection of light of the badge on the jacket.

The badge reads "Sheriff".

                    SHERIFF
          God dammit, not again. Wake up boy.
          Jacob! Wake up!

                                              CUT TO:

INT. SALOON - NIGHT

Jacob comes out of his flashback and back to reality.

He grunts and tries to focus his eyes.

Slowly things come to focus.

More shuffling and grunting and cursing.

Feeling starts coming back to Jacob in nauseating waves.

He is careful not to groan or call out but to seem still.

He sees men loading other bodies onto a small boat.

He watches as one man, BLACK PETE, walks back and stands
right in front of him.

He turns and bends down to lift another body and Jacob sees a
small dagger tucked into the man's boot.

Suddenly he reaches for the knife, clutching the man by both
legs.

Pete kicks and cries out.

Gundersen drops the body and comes over.

Jacob tries to get to his feet, but the men start beating
him.

They both land blows until Jacob collapses in a ball.

Gundersen grabs his shoulders to lift him up.

Suddenly, Jacob thrusts out with the dagger he had concealed
and stabs Gundersen in the eye.

Gundersen screams as he falls, clutching his eye.

Pete pulls out a large knife and leaps on Jacob.

They struggle with the knife until Pete has the knife down
and presses into Jacob's side.

The blade starts to go in. Jacob screams and Pete leans into it, smiling a hideous gold-toothed grin.

Jacob screams with his mouth wide and his head thrown back. Pete presses the knife in further and leans in closer.

Suddenly, Jacob bursts his head forward and bites Pete's nose off with a wet crunch.

Pete loosens his grip on the knife and Jacob rolls away.

Pete rolls on the floor holding his nose and screaming as blood gushes out of his face.

Jacob stands and pulls the knife from his side with a grunt.

He drops it, then spits a bloody gob of flesh out onto the ground.

Pete's nose floats in a bloody pool of spit.

Jacob staggers out of the hold and into the blinding sunrise.

EXT. STABLE - MORNING

Jacob packs his saddlebags. He stops, seeing a bucket lying in a corner near a trough.

He grabs a bucket and dunks his head in, rinses away some of the blood. He rinses his mouth and spits.

Bill comes out to get his horse. He stops when he sees Jacob.

He looks at Jacob, stunned. Then, he smiles a widely and chuckles.

                    BILL
          Jesus man, what the hell happened
          to you? You like you had a worse
          night than me.

                    JACOB
          I'll tell you all about it. As soon
          as we get on he road.

Bill laughs and slaps Jacob on the back.

INT. TSE-WHIT-ZEN VILLAGE, LONGHOUSE - NIGHT

Siya sits by a fire. Several others lay asleep on the floor on mats, bundled in fur blankets.

Siya looks into the fire as he slowly and methodically carves on a small piece of bone.

As his hands move rhythmically with the knife, he hums a soft chant under his breath.

Suddenly, dogs begin to bark and Siya looks up sharply.

People start to rouse. One man jumps up and grabs a spear. Another man opens the large wooden door at the front of the longhouse.

EXT. TSE-WHIT-ZEN VILLAGE - NIGHT

Siya and some other men exit the tent and step out into the clear, cold night.

Dogs bark at the edge of the village, which is situated near the top of the beach line.

Two men with spears in their hands run up to the dogs as they start to bark louder.

They stare intently for a moment into the darkness.

Suddenly, the dogs take off at a run into the dark, tall grass.

Siya stands behind TIK-WO-TAN, the chief, as they wait for the two men and dogs to reappear.

The barking stops and the men walk out of the grass with a third man between them, an arm supported by each man on either side.

As they approach, the man in the middle, Chuka, breaks off and steps toward Siya. He stops in front of him.

> SIYA
> So, my son, you have returned.

He smiles and steps up and embraces him.

> SIYA
> (quietly)
> And I sense that the spirits have
> changed you.

He unhooks from the embrace and holds Siya at arms length.

People start to gather around and question and talk quietly as they press in to hear the exchange.

                    SIYA
          This is my grandson, Chuka, who
          left us to seek the guidance and
          power of the great spirits, as his
          father and father's father have
          done before him.

Siya smiles at Chuka. Others murmur sounds of approval.

                    SIYA
          Now, he has returned to us. No
          longer a boy, but a man. Stand
          before us now, son, and tell us
          what the spirits revealed to you.
          Tell us who you are and we will
          sing your song with respect and
          honor.

Chuka steps back and smiles tiredly at his grandfather. He is
muddy, scratched, and exhausted.

He turns and looks at the people pressed together in a half
circle, smiling and waiting for his reply.

                    CHUKA
          Thank you, Siya, I have sought the
          voices of the spirits. I have asked
          them to bless me with a power that
          will help our people, protect us,
          and keep us strong. I had to go
          farther than any have gone, to the
          very pulsing heart of the river. I
          was guided there by my father's
          spirit, and with the great spirit,
          together they led me to a magic
          place. A place where the water was
          alive with the great spirit and
          full of deep magic and power.

There were awed murmurs from the crowd. Siya nodded gravely
and looked at Chuka.

                    SIYA
          Did you touch the magic water?

More murmurs as everyone looks at Chuka expectantly.

                    CHUKA
          Yes. I was drawn to the water, into
          a shallow pool. I was almost dead
          from exhaustion and not having
          taken in any food for many days as
          I followed the river up the
          mountain.
                    (MORE)

                         CHUKA (CONT'D)
          The water was alive with healing
          spirits, and it made me whole
          again. It filled me with a power
          that wiped away all hunger and
          exhaustion and it made me whole.
          The voice of my father sang to me
          in the pool, and I promised him to
          use this power for the good of my
          people.

Siya steps close again and puts his hands on Chuka's
shoulders. He looks into his eyes intently.

                         SIYA
          Chuka left us as a boy, and in his
          place a man has returned. This is
          my grandson, now named Chuk-wa-tal,
          and he is a man. Chuk-wa-tal, we
          honor you this night.

He lifts his head to the stars and begins a soulful singing,
chanting. He raises his arms to the sky as his voice grows
louder and stronger.

Soon, there are many voices singing. The soulful voices fill
the night air.

A man stands in the shadow of a doorway to a small hut and
watches the singing group silently. He grunts then closes the
door gruffly.

EXT. ROAD - DAY

Jacob and Bill ride side-by-side down a winding trail through
giant trees.

Bill looks sideways at Jacob, who is dabbing at a cut on his
left cheek with a handkerchief.

He spits blood and reaches into his mouth. He twists his hand
for a moment, then pulls out a bloody tooth.

He looks at it grimly then tosses it aside.

                         JACOB
          So, I'm guessing you're surprised
          to see me this morning.

He looks at Bill coldly.

                         JACOB
          You could have warned me.

Bill looks back sharply for a moment, then laughs softly.

                    BILL
          I thought I did.

Jacob stares sullenly for a moment then grunts. Then, he
sighs and spits more blood.

                    JACOB
          Well, you could have been a little
          more specific.

                    BILL
          I thought a sharp young fellow,
          especially a deputy from San
          Fransisco would be well aware of
          the crimper's game. I thought you
          could take care of yourself.

He smiles broadly.

                    BILL
          And it seems I wasn't altogether
          wrong on that count, now was I?

Jacob looks at him and grunts again. A faint smile curls his
lips.

                    JACOB
          I'm not from San Fransisco, I said
          a small town just outside the city.
          But, I am familiar with evil men...
          and their ways. I guess I just...
          got caught off guard.

                    BILL
          Well, don't be too hard on
          yourself, laddy. You are still
          here. Quite a feat to tell you
          truly. I imagine miss Frankie will
          be none too happy to see you around
          any time soon. They'll be looking
          for you.

                    JACOB
          I've got a few words of my own for
          her.

Bill looks at Jacob, then laughs again, heartily.

                    BILL
          I bet you do, laddy, I bet you do.
          But, I'd put those thoughts out of
          your head for a bit.
                    (MORE)

                    BILL (CONT'D)
          You've got some healing up to do
          first and we've got a good spell of
          work to cure you. Sides', round
          here a man needs friends if he
          expects to survive.

Jacob says nothing, just stares ahead.

INT. TSE-WHIT-ZEN VILLAGE - EARLY MORNING

Inside a longhouse people are sleeping on mats wrapped in fur
blankets. Chuk-wa-tal is asleep.

A woman's terrible scream rips the air and his eyes pop open.
He jumps out of bed as others do too, and stumbles for the
door as people start to rouse and investigate the screams.

As he steps out in front of the longhouse, a man and a crying
woman step out of a nearby hut with a man in their arms.

His head has a bloody gash across it. He is dead.

More cries as people wake and more bodies are found.

Tik-wo-tan, the chief, comes out of the longhouse. SIK-WAY, a
warrior, runs up breathlessly.

                    SIK-WAY
          Chief, we were raided last night.
          Four men are dead and five people
          are missing. Two children and three
          girls. It looks like it was a
          Cowichan party, it must have been a
          small group. They fed poisoned meat
          to the dogs, that's why there was
          no alarm. All but three died. The
          others will be sick for a time, but
          will live.

                    TIK-WO-TAN
          Gather the elders. We must be
          decide what to do now and act
          quickly.

                    SIK-WAY
          There is something else. One of the
          girls that was taken...

He looks down, ashamed, not knowing how to say the words
right.

Tik-wo-tan looks at him then his eyes understand. He looks
around.

                    TIK-WO-TAN
          Elta? Where's Elta?

                    SIK-WAY
          Your daughter... the Princess was
          taken.

INT. TSE-WHIT-ZEN VILLAGE - DAY

Tik-wo-tan, Siya, Chuk-wa-tal, Sik-way, and other elders are
seated in the longhouse around the fire.

                    TIK-WO-TAN
          Are we sure it was a Cowichan
          raiding party?

                    SIK-WAY
          We found this, it must have been
          torn off by one of the captives as
          they were taken. They must have
          been in such a hurry to get out
          quietly that they left it.

He holds out a carved wooden mask, a grotesque figure with
protruding eyes and a long curved beak like nose.

                    TIK-WO-TAN
          Swaihwe.

Tik-wo-tan takes the mask and holds it up. It has fresh
scratch marks on one side. He looks at the group.

                    TIK-WO-TAN
          How many canoes can be ready by
          nightfall?

                    SIK-WAY
          At least 20. I'll send runners up
          the river to the fishing camps. If
          they move fast enough, we may get
          more.

                    SIYA
          To bring Swaihwe on a night raid...
          that is very bold for a small party
          trying to avoid a fight. Why would
          they be so careless?

He looks at the other men calmly, with a slight smile.

                    SIYA
          Chuk-wa-tal, what do think of this?
          You have just come from talking
          with the spirits. Maybe you can
          still hear their voices enough to
          find the truth of these things?

All eyes turn towards Chuk-wa-tal, and he looks back
nervously.

                    CHUK-WA-TAL
          Well, I... Maybe it wasn't.

                    SIK-WAY
          Wasn't, wasn't what?

                    CHUK-WA-TAL
          I mean, maybe it wasn't the
          Cowichan. Maybe someone left the
          mask on purpose, so we would think
          it was a Cowichan raid?

Siya smiles wider and nods slightly. He seems to be
satisfied.

The others seem unconvinced. Sik-way seems to be enraged by
this idea.

                    SIK-WAY
          Who would play such a trick? And
          why? That is a coward's game.

Sik-way stands threateningly.

                    SIK-WAY
          And only a coward's mind would
          think of such things!

Chuk-wa-tal flushes with anger and embarrassment.

                    CHUK-WA-TAL
          It was just a thought.

He stands slowly.

                    CHUK-WA-TAL
          And I'm no coward. I will help
          protect our people.

                    SIK-WAY
          How? By bathing us in magic water?
          We need warriors not foolish ideas.

40.

Tik-wo-tan stands and puts his arms between the two in a
gesture of restraint.

He looks at them in turn.

                    TIK-WO-TAN
          We need both of you, and we need
          you working as brothers,not as
          enemies.

He looks at Chuk-wa-tal.

                    TIK-WO-TAN
          I do agree with Sik-way though, it
          seems an unlikely idea. Who would
          do such a thing? And why? And we do
          need to be strong for our people,
          and to show we cannot be taken from
          easily, or without consequence.

Siya stands as well.

                    SIYA
          Maybe it would be wise to think
          more on these things. I think we
          should go talk to the White
          Marshall. He will know if anyone is
          stirring up trouble.

                    TIK-WO-TAN
          We have to act now, tonight.

                    SIYA
          Rash action would only feed into
          someone's plot, if they were
          leading us astray. What would
          killing innocent people do to help
          us?

                    SIK-WAY
          The Cowichan aren't innocent, even
          if they didn't do this. They are
          our enemies. How many times have
          they raided us, taken our children
          as captives?

                    SIYA
          And how many times did they bring
          Swaihwe? Or poison dogs?

                    SIK-WAY
          Their growing boldness is a sign
          that they think we are weak.
                    (MORE)

                    SIK-WAY (CONT'D)
          That's even more reason to strike
          now, and strike hard.

The men stare at each other for a long moment. Tik-wo-tan
finally sighs heavily.

                    TIK-WO-TAN
          Alright, we'll wait one day. Siya
          and Sik-way will go into the White
          Man's Village tomorrow and talk to
          the Marshall. If we find no hidden
          enemy, we attack tomorrow night. In
          the mean time, get every canoe from
          all the fishing camps here by
          tomorrow.

                    SIYA
          I'd like Chuk-wa-tal to come with
          us.

Tik-wo-tan looks at Siya. He nods slightly. They all start to
leave slowly.

Tik-wo-tan puts a hand on Sik-way's shoulder softly and leans
in behind him. He holds a small object wrapped in a skin out
to Sik-way down low, so no one can see.

Sik-way takes it and looks at him.

                    TIK-WO-TAN
          Take this to the woman named
          Frankie at the Inn. She will have a
          package for you to bring back.

Sik-way looks at him eagerly. He smiles crookedly.

                    SIK-WAY
          Does this mean--

                    TIK-WO-TAN
             (cutting him off)
          It means I want my daughter back,
          and I'm not taking any chances this
          time.

EXT. ROAD - SUNSET

Bill and Jacob ride in a single file. Bill is now in the
lead. Ahead, the sun is setting through a break in the
thickly forested road, lighting them with a brilliant orange-
pink glow.

Bill comes out of the forest into an opening on a hillside
and stops.

As Jacob rides up beside him, he sees the sun setting behind
a forested hill that dives down to meet the water.

A line of smoke comes from a group of small buildings on a
long pier hugging the water's edge.

They both look in silence for a long moment.

Bill turns with a broad grin towards Jacob and gives him a
hearty slap on the back.

> BILL
> What'ya think then, Jake? It look
> like what you're after? A fresh
> start?

He laughs.

> BILL
> C'mon then. Let's introduce Port
> Crescent to the man who got away
> from miss Frankie's crimper. I'm
> sure you'll have no trouble getting
> a whiskey here tonight.

Bill rides ahead down the hill towards Port Crescent.

Jacob stares at the sunset for a moment, then takes out a
worn piece of paper.

He looks at it. He looks up at the small port town clinging
to the hillside, swallowed up on all side by giant trees.

He smiles.

> JACOB
> (quietly, to himself)
> Yeah, I think it is.

As he rides away to catch up to Bill, the paper drops from
his hand and lands on the muddy road.

PAPER - "FREE LAND! COME TO WASHINGTON TERRITORY!"

EXT. FOREST - DUSK

A man is at the base of a giant tree, laying out his tools
and preparing to cut it down.

He picks up a large axe and lines himself up to take a swing.

He looks up the giant tree as he holds the axe in both hands, blade just touching the place where his first blow will land.

He pulls back his arms in a wide arc and bring the axe down in a massive blow.

As the axe strikes the tree, there is an explosion of fir needles and branches snapping from above.

He lets out a startled cry and steps back, axe still stuck in the tree as a giant dark figure swings out from a large branch just above his head. The dark figure leaps out and catches a branch in the next tree.

The dark figure wears a dark fur that is covered in fir needles. He swings through the trees like a gorilla or large ape.

The man stares, horror-stricken for a long moment, then runs away, leaving his tools and the large axe still stuck in the tree.

INT. LOGGING CAMP, BUNKHOUSE - NIGHT

A large wooden bunkhouse with one open room lined with bunk beds on three sides.

A large potbelly wood stove sits in the center, around which are twenty or so men are strewn about on bunks and sitting on cut rounds of wood for stools.

They play cards, read, drink, and smoke.

Suddenly, the small wooden door flies open and the man, EMIL, bursts in, panting and out of breath.

Men start to murmur and sit up, aware something is amiss.

CHARLES SWANSON, a large burly man with a walrus mustache, stands and takes a step toward Emil, who is still panting, eyes wide with terror.

                    SWANSON
          Emil, what the devil's a' matter?
          Christ, you look like you seen some
          kind a' ghost.

Swanson steps closer and grabs Emil by the shoulder and looks into his wide eyed face. He helps him to a block of wood by the fire.

                    SWANSON
          By god man, what happened to you?

Turning to speak to the other men

                    SWANSON
          Bring us a dram of whiskey, some
          hot water, and the lemon extract,
          quickly now!

Men shuffle quickly behind them and in a moment the items
appear from several rough hands.

Swanson takes the flask of whiskey and pours a healthy amount
in the mug of hot water. Then, he mixes in the lemon powder
and stirs a few quick times.

He leans in to Emil.

                    SWANSON
          Here now, drink this straight down.

He hands the steaming cup to Emil, who slowly takes it.

Emil holds it under his nose for a moment, then finally his
look of terror relaxes and he closes his eyes.

                    SWANSON
          That's it, drink it right down, all
          of it now.

Emil slowly starts to drink, then lifts it high and finishes
with a gasp.

He pants for a few seconds as color returns to his face and
finally his eyes seem to focus.

                    SWANSON
          That's it, man. Now, tell us what
          in the name of the holy mother
          scared the wits out of you so bad.

Emil closes his eyes for a moment, then opens them and looks
down. He starts to speak slowly in a voice heavily accented
in German.

                    EMIL
          I vas in ze cut, making von final
          pass before I done for ze day. I
          see good fir tree, tall, straight,
          but not too big. I think I fall it
          myself before nightfall. Easy vork.
          Good vork. But ven I strike ze
          tree...

He stops, the terrified look coming back.

                         SWANSON
              What man? What happened?

                          EMIL
              Great hairy beast look like a man
              come out of branches like ze devil
              him selv.

Everyone is silent and seems to be holding their breath,
waiting to hear more.

Suddenly, Emil stands, almost knocking over the two men
beside him as they shrink back startled.

He looks up with blazing eyes as if he just realized what he
needed to do.

                          EMIL
              I no vork here no more!

He rushes to a bunk on the side of the cabin and hurriedly
bundles up some loose belongings.

He turns and stops for a moment, looking at the bewildered
faces around him.

He talks in a hushed voice, almost a whisper.

                          EMIL
              It vas him. It vas ze vild man.

He heads for the door and exits as quickly as he had entered.

The men look at each other and all eyes turn to Swanson.

Swanson looks grim. He takes a pull of whiskey from the flask
still in his hand.

                         SWANSON
              Alright boys, settle down. I'm
              going to town tomorrow to see the
              Marshall. If it was Turnow, we'll
              get some dogs up here... and we'll
              go get the som' bitch.

EXT. PORT CRESCENT - SUNSET

Bill and Jacob ride into PORT CRESCENT, a small group of
wooden buildings clinging to the shoreline beneath a freshly
denuded hillside.

As they enter into town, a small hand painted sign greets
them.

46.

It reads - "Welcome to Port Crescent, the largest logging
works in the world!"

Jacob smiles slightly, then looks at Bill.

                    JACOB
          That true?

Bill looks back at him and grins slyly.

                    BILL
          Well, as long as you're in camp,
          you'd better make like it is. This
          is Old man Lehman's dirty little
          paradise and he likes all his
          grubby little angels to sing him
          sweet praise, if you get my drift.

Jacob stares at him, deadpan. He grunts.

Bill stops his horse and Jacob does the same.

                    BILL
          As a matter of fact, I have some
          business with the old man, and I
          guess you'll be need'n to meet him
          sooner rather than later, based on
          certain rumors that are sure to
          flying around. Side's, best time to
          strike is when the iron's hot, so
          they say. I'll tell him I'll take
          you to camp with me. I can use
          another strong back on the rigging
          crew.

                    JACOB
          Sounds fair. Thank you, Bill. I
          appreciate your helpin' me out like
          this.

Bill chuckles. He snaps his reigns and starts off again.

                    BILL
          Well, I think you should spend a
          few days on the crew first before
          you get too grateful. You'll have
          to earn your own way. I won't lie
          about that.

                    JACOB
          Fair enough. Now, let's go meet
          this old boss of yours.

                    BILL
          You mean your new boss.

They approach the largest building in town, a big rectangular
building with a long covered porch facing the boardwalk.

A sign on the front reads - "Markham House".

Lively sounds come from within, where twinkles of candlelight
can be seen through the wavy glass windows.

INT. MARKHAM HOUSE - NIGHT

A man is sitting in a small, but richly-decorated office.

Survey maps and railroad platens cover the walls. Big mounted
elk and deer heads hang on the walls.

The man, ED LEHMAN, co-owner of the camp town of Port
Crescent, is a large man with a bald head and a bushy
mustache.

He sits behind the desk with a paper in front of him as well
as a glass of whiskey.

In his mouth, he smokes a large brier pipe. A thin line of
smoke curls up from it.

He writes quickly, seeming to be in a hurry to get words on
paper as fast as possible.

A knock comes st the door.

Lehman stops mid-letter and looks up sharply, irritated. The
ink bleeds where he stops.

                    LEHMAN
          Damn! What?!

A voice comes from outside the door.

                    BILL
          It's me, Hatch.

Lehman curses to himself then quickly shuffles the paper,
pen, and ink into a drawer.

He sits back and takes the pipe from his mouth and taps it
out into an ashtray on his desk.

                    LEHMAN
          Come in then, come in.

48.

Bill shuffles in and Jacob follows. Lehman eyes him with mild
amusement, but not seemingly surprised.

He waves a hand toward the two chairs in front of his desk.

>   LEHMAN
>   Sit, both of you.

They sit. Lehman looks at them and chuckles.

He pulls out a small tin of tobacco and opens it. He loads
his pipe, then lights it with a large wooden match.

He smiles at them.

>   LEHMAN
>   So, this must be the man with the
>   appetite for dark meat, eh? I would
>   have paid dearly to see that show,
>   I must admit. It would have given a
>   whole new meaning to the term
>   dinner theater, I'm sure.

He laughs again and Jacob looks flushed, clearly not amused.

Bill looks at Jacob questioningly.

>   LEHMAN
>   You haven't heard the story yet,
>   Hatch?
>   (laughs)
>   And you had that nice little ride
>   together all day to swap war
>   stories. Well, Mr. Miller, I guess
>   you're the silent type, then? That
>   pirating crimper, Buster Kelly,
>   isn't so shy, and his men who you
>   messed up had plenty to say about
>   you. Word is spreading like
>   wildfire to every port in the
>   territory that there is a deranged
>   cowboy, maybe even a cannibal,
>   praying on helpless sailors
>   stalking the saloons of the
>   peninsula. I hear talk the union
>   boss is even going to put a reward
>   on your head. They're probably
>   drawing the wanted posters as we
>   speak.

Jacob is tense. He glances at Bill who looks back at him.

Lehman looks at Jacob closely, then puts out his hand.

>   LEHMAN
>   So, Mr. Miller, I'd like to shake
>   your hand.

Jacob looks at him carefully and then at Bill again. Bill smiles broadly.

>   LEHMAN
>   Anyone who can shake those bastards
>   up so damn good has my respect,
>   sir. Whiskey is on the house
>   tonight.

Jacob takes the hand reluctantly.

>   JACOB
>   Look, I don't want to get caught up
>   in any trouble. I was just trying
>   to protect myself. I didn't aim to
>   do any harm to anyone.

Lehman chuckles again and leans back, puffing on his pipe.

>   LEHMAN
>   He's humble, too. Looks like you
>   found us a genuine cowboy, Hatch.
>   So, what's your plan then, cowboy?
>   What can a humble log baron do for
>   you besides provide a warm bed and
>   some stiff drink for the night?

Jacob stiffens his jaw and says nothing for an awkward moment. Bill glances at him, then speaks.

>   BILL
>   I need another man on the rigging
>   crew up at camp four. I'd like to
>   take him up in the morning, if he'd
>   like to earn an honest day's pay.

All eyes turn on Jacob. He sighs.

>   JACOB
>   Yes, sir. All I'm looking for is an
>   honest chance, same as anyone else.
>   I can earn my keep.

>   LEHMAN
>   They say you were a lawman down
>   south. I'm guessing you have no
>   experience or skills with lumber?

Jacob stares at him. Lehman stares back.

50.

>   BILL
>   I can show him the ropes. I'm sure
>   he's a quick learner.

>   LEHMAN
>   Oh, I'm sure he is.

INT. SALOON, TRACY'S BEDROOM - DAY

Tracy, the prostitute, sits on the edge of her bed. She
looks into a small dirty mirror.

She is carefully applying powdered makeup over the small cut
on her lower lip.

She looks in the mirror at herself, then starts as she sees a
woman in the reflection behind her.

She turns and looks at her with a scared expression for a
second, then smiles weakly.

>   TRACY
>   Frankie, I didn't hear you. Come
>   in, have a seat.

Frankie, the madame, comes in and walks slowly around the
edge of the room, not looking at Tracy, but seeming to
examine all her meager belongings.

She reaches a shelf holding candles and a prayer book. Her
hand traces over the top.

Tracy looks back into the mirror nervously and continues
applying makeup.

>   FRANKIE
>   Tell me, Tracy, what do you see
>   when you look in there?

Tracy stops and looks at Frankie nervously.

>   TRACY
>   What do you mean? My reflection?

Frankie picks up the prayer book and holds it gently. She
turns toward Tracy and slowly walks toward her.

>   FRANKIE
>   I mean, look into that mirror, and
>   tell me what you see in there.

Tracy still looks up at Frankie as she comes to her and sits
slowly beside her.

She sets the prayer book on her lap. She reaches up and
softly caresses Tracy's cheek as she speaks.

                    TRACY
          Frankie... I don't...

Frankie traces her hand down her neck slowly.

                    FRANKIE
          Shhh... hush now...

She touches her fingers softly to Tracy's lips. Tracy
trembles.

Frankie leans close to Tracy's ear.

                    FRANKIE
          I'll tell you what I see. A
          beautiful, strong, lovely... whore.
          Not a lady, not a wife, not a
          mother, but a two-cent whore who
          will never be anything more or
          anything less. A cheap, dirty fuck.

She grabs Tracy by the hair now and pulls back savagely.

Tracy lets out a small whimper then bites her lip as tears
roll down her cheeks.

                    FRANKIE
          You let me down last night, Tracy.
          And I had such high hopes for you.
          But, for some reason, you seem to
          be smitten by that ragged old
          Irishman. Stupid bitch. You think
          he cares about you at all?

Frankie pulls harder and Tracy lets out a small cry.

                    TRACY
          Frankie, please! I--

                    FRANKIE
          Shut up!

Frankie cuts her off with a savage blow with the prayer book
to her face.

She lets her go and Tracy drops to the bed, face bleeding
from a large cut over one eye.

Frankie looks at her with a cruel smile. She holds the book
in her hand, testing the weight.

52.

                              FRANKIE
                    Oh my. I didn't mean to strike so
                    hard. This book feels awfully heavy
                    for such a little thing. Must be
                    some big prayers in here, huh?

Tracy looks up, but says nothing.

Frankie slowly opens the book to reveal a small pistol, a
derringer.

She take it out and drops the book. She looks at it with mock
surprise and holds it up like it's going to bite her.

                              FRANKIE
                    A gun! And you know my rules about
                    whores keeping guns in my place.
                    Oh, sweetheart, such a shame.

She holds the gun in her open palm, butt facing out. Slowly
she grips the barrel and looks down at Tracy.

She gently brushes the hair away from Tracy's bloody face.

Tracy looks at her with blazing eyes, still crying.

                              TRACY
                    Frankie, you don't understand...
                    please, I'm sorry.

                              FRANKIE
                    I know you are sweetie. I know you
                    are.

Tracy lets out a short scream as Frankie brings the butt of
the small pistol down in a hard swing into her face.

INT. MARSHAL'S OFFICE - DAY

MARSHAL HOWARD DEAN, a rough and no-nonsense man dressed in
plain clothes with a large black wool coat that holds a large
star pinned to the left lapel that reads US TERRITORY
MARSHAL, sits in a chair behind a small empty wooden desk.

DEPUTY COLIN MCKENZIE, a young man with a mess of hair under
a large brimmed hat, sits staring out the dirty front
windows, chewing sloppily on a wad of tobacco.

Deputy McKenzie stands suddenly, and turns to Marshal with a
mischievous grin, brown saliva running down his chin.

                    MCKENZIE
          Marshal, we got us some ingins'
          coming in. Three ugly mothers if I
          ever seen em'. I got this, don't
          worry.

Without waiting for a reply, the eager deputy steps outside,
grabbing a shotgun by the door as he does.

McKenzie steps outside right as Siya, Sik-way, and Chuk-wa-
tal are approaching the door.

He lays the gun on his crossed arms.

                    MCKENZIE
          That's far enough now. You boys
          must not have heard the new law
          Judge Smith passed in town after
          the massacre your fellows did last
          winter?

The three men stop and look at him. Sik-way looks furious and
moves to step forward, one hand gripping his spear, but Siya
puts a restraining hand on his chest. Siya looks at McKenzie
calmly as the deputy cocks both barrels of the shotgun and
aims it at the center of the group.

                    SIYA
               (in English)
          What law is that, Deputy?

McKenzie grins a tobacco slime grin.

                    MCKENZIE
          We call it the "War Party Law."
          See, we can't trust you dirty
          savages no more than a wild pack of
          dogs. So any more than three
          savages in town together officially
          makes a war party. And that
          officially gives me the right to
          cut you down in the street on
          sight, like the savage dogs you
          are. What you think about that,
          Chief?

McKenzie spits a slimy brown glob and steps forward off the
steps.

The three men don't move, but Chuk-wa-tal grabs Siya on the
arm in reflex.

McKenzie laughs. A loud voice comes from the doorway behind
him.

                    MARSHAL
          Back down, deputy... these men are
          peaceful. They mean no violence.

The Deputy holds his gun for a moment, then lifts it with a
wicked grin. He steps away to the side.

                    MCKENZIE
          Hell Marshal, I's just givin him a
          bad time. I didn't mean nothin' by
          it. Hell, I'm peaceful too.

He smiles a twisted choir-boy smile.

Marshal grunts and looks at McKenzie like a child who just
misbehaved.

He holds the door open.

                    MARSHAL
          Come on in, boys, have a seat.
          McKenzie, close the door behind us
          and wait outside.

They walk inside, Marshal sits on his desk and the three men
stand in front of him.

He sighs.

                    MARSHAL
          Okay. Now, what is it that I can do
          for you fellas? I hope there hasn't
          been any trouble in the village.

                    SIYA
          Raiding party last night. Four
          dead, five taken.

                    MARSHAL
          Shit. Okay, any ideas what tribe
          this time?

                    SIK-WAY
               (in English)
          Cowichan.

Marshal looks at him.

                    SIYA
          Or, someone who make it look like
          Cowichan.

Marshal looks between them for a moment, studying both faces.
He nods his slow understanding.

                    MARSHAL
          So, you think someone might be
          posing as Cowichan, and raiding
          local tribes?

Siya stares at him but says nothing.

                    MARSHAL
          And you think it must be some white
          boys, that's why you came to me?
          Thought maybe some boys may be
          braggin' about their little dress
          up party in the saloon last night,
          that sort of thing?

Still Siya says nothing, makes no response.

Marshal steps closer.

                    MARSHAL
          Let me tell you something, Chief--

                    CHUK-WA-TAL
               (in English)
          He's not the Chief.

Marshal turns his sharp eyes on Chuk-wa-tal.

                    MARSHAL
          And who might you be?

                    CHUK-WA-TAL
          No one.

                    MARSHAL
          And what may I ask, makes you think
          it was a couple white boys and not
          just another tribe trying to
          confuse you? Or maybe it was the
          Cowichan, like stone face here
          thinks.

He gestures at Sik-way, who scowls at him.

He looks at them for a moment, then sighs and rubs his face.

He turns and sits back down at his chair. He looks at the
group tiredly.

                    MARSHAL
          Look, boys, the truth is I don't
          give two shits if you all run round
          clubbing and taking each other
          until you all disappeared.
                    (MORE)

                    MARSHAL (CONT'D)
          And neither does anyone else in
          town. What happens in your village
          is your own problem, not mine.

                    SIYA
          But, what white men do, even in our
          village, is your problem.

                    MARSHAL
          And what in the hell would any
          white boys want with killing and
          stealing Indians? I'm sorry, it
          just don't make sense.

They stand and stare at each other. Sik-way glares at Siya
angrily.

Marshal sighs again.

                    MARSHAL
          Do I make myself clear, or do you
          not understand me?

Siya looks at him closely.

                    SIYA
          What will you do if it is whites?

Marshal shakes his head.

                    MARSHAL
          God damn, you're a stubborn old
          goat, aint' you Chief?

Marshal stands and walks to the door, opens it.

                    MARSHAL
          You best forget about wild ideas
          you may have. They're bound to get
          you into trouble. Unless you catch
          a white man red-handed in a crime
          in your village, I don't want to
          hear about anymore of this talk.
          This is the kind of thing that's
          bound to stir up the hornet's nest
          if you're not careful.

The Native men exit and the Deputy and Marshal watch them go.

EXT. MARSHAL'S OFFICE - DAY

As the men walk away, Chuk-wa-tal looks at Siya.

                    CHUK-WA-TAL
          Why provoke him? What does that
          gain us?

                    SIK-WAY
          This was a fool's errand. We should
          be launching the war canoes, not
          wasting time with talking to white
          men.

                    SIYA
          Perhaps. But, a seed may take root
          even in hostile soil, if wisely
          planted.

Sik-way grunts, disgusted.

Siya looks at him.

                    SIYA
          Sik-way is right, though. We must
          get back right away. There is no
          time to waste. The tide is going
          out, we will walk down the beach.

Sik-way stops and turns. The others look at him, surprised.

He looks flushed.

                    SIK-WAY
          I will stay and have a drink. At
          least while I'm here I can enjoy
          one of the only good things the
          white man has.

He grunts again then turns and leaves quickly. They watch him
go.

EXT. BEACH - DAY

Siya and Chuk-wa-tal walk along the beach together.

                    CHUK-WA-TAL
          Don't you think it's strange that
          he wanted to stay? Wouldn't he go
          to lead the charge and gloat that
          he was right? This makes no sense,
          Siya.

Siya looks at him and nods smiling slightly.

58.

                    SIYA
          You are right and you are wrong. It
          is strange, but not everything
          always makes sense. You just have
          to have wiser eyes to see with. In
          time, my son. All things in time.

They continue down the beach together, towards the setting
sun.

INT. SALOON - NIGHT

The Olympian House main saloon is large, open room with
exposed timber rafters on the inside and a large deer antler
chandelier with a stage on the far wall.

On stage, three women in bawdy dress dance to the fast-paced
rhythm of a ragtime piano, played by a thin young man just in
front of the stage.

On either side of the large open dance floor are small wooden
tables and chairs filled with dirty men drinking, smoking,
gambling, and talking loudly.

A long wooden bar of a solid rough hewn log sits behind the
tables on one side.

Swanson walks in and approaches a table in a far corner where
Marshal and Deputy McKenzie sit, drinking from tall mugs of
flat beer.

Marshal looks up at him with cold eyes as he approaches.

McKenzie grins stupidly and spits a slimy wad into a brass
pot on the floor.

It hits with a ringing splat and brown slime dribbles down
his chin.

                    MCKENZIE
          Marshal's done for the day, boy.
          You need to see him, you come by
          the office in the morning.

Swanson takes off his hat and looks at Marshal.

                    SWANSON
          Beggin' your pardon, Marshal, but
          I'm just come down from the high
          camp up at Sawtooth Ridge.

He rubs the back of his neck nervously and looks at his
boots.

                    SWANSON
          Well, we had a man leave camp in
          hysterics last night, and... well,
          I think it may be Turnow.

Marshal sighs, takes a long swig of beer, and kicks out a
chair in front of him.

                    MARSHAL
          Have a seat.

Swanson sits and Marshal takes another swig of beer, then
looks at Swanson.

                    MARSHAL
          What's your name?

                    SWANSON
          Swanson, sir. Charles Swanson. I'm
          the boss up at camp three.

Marshal and McKenzie study him. Swanson looks back nervously.

Marshal takes another long swig. Swanson watches and licks
his dry lips.

                    MCKENZIE
          Spit it out now, boy, we ain't got
          all night.

Marshal looks at McKenzie out of the corner of his eye and
sighs.

                    SWANSON
          Right, so, um, we had a man leave
          camp in a fit last night. He near
          lost his damn mind he was so
          scar't. Made all the boys pucker up
          tight too. Got em' spooked near
          witless, to tell the truth.

                    MARSHAL
          And this man, he saw Turnow?

                    SWANSON
          Well, he saw... something.
          Something big, and he said...

Swanson rubs his neck again nervously and then looks from
McKenzie to Marshal. They stare back, waiting.

On stage, the dancers twirl and bounce to the plinking piano
music.

Swanson swallows.

                    SWANSON
          He said he seen something in the
          tree he was fellin'. Something like
          a wild beast man that swung out
          through the branches and
          disappeared like a ghost. He said
          it was big as a large man and wild
          as an ape. I 'membered what was
          told when they chased Turnow up
          Oxbow. They said there was no
          tracks to and from his camp. One
          fella figured he must a been using
          the trees like an ape.

Swanson looks at them, evidently done with his story.

Marshal stares at the girls on stage for a moment, then
sighs, slowly looking back to Swanson.

                    MARSHAL
          So what can I do for you?

                    SWANSON
          Well.. I's hopin'...

                    MARSHAL
          You were hoping I'd round up a
          posse and head up to Sawtooth
          Ridge, torches blazing?

Swanson flushes in frustration.

Marshal takes on final swig of his beer and drains it.

                    MARSHAL
          And what if I told you two days ago
          a similar story came up from
          Aberdeen? And five days before
          that, a camp deacon out in the
          Simpson camps swore he saw Turnow
          stalking the camp late at night.
          Says he killed three chickens and a
          dog. This five thousand dollar
          reward has caused Turnow fever to
          break out from Olympia to Tacoma,
          not to mention the whole damn
          Olympic Peninsula. But, so far the
          only real evidence we have is those
          two boys he shot dead last year.
          Since then, not a single report
          among the thousands that have
          flooded in has led to the man.
                    (MORE)

                    MARSHAL (CONT'D)
          Every trapper and crackpot in the
          Territory is prowling the hills
          dreaming of that reward, and still
          eleven months later, no Turnow.

Marshal sighs, then puts out his cigar. He stands.

                    MARSHAL
          I can't afford to chase after ghost
          stories, Mr. Swanson. Now, if
          you'll excuse me.

He nods to the Deputy then walks off.

Swanson watches him go and curses. McKenzie looks at him.

He smiles, and spits into the spittoon again.

                    MCKENZIE
          Hell boy, Marshal ain't got time to
          chase the bogeyman around the in
          the foothills. And he sure don't
          want no loonies stirring up a posse
          over nothin'. Hell, what you need
          is a tracker. Someone with a couple
          good hounds that can sneak in,
          quiet like. Side's, if he is there,
          you think twenty fools with blazing
          torches wouldn't scare the man
          away? Why'd you think he ain't been
          caught yet? No, what you need is a
          partner, a man that knows the
          manhunt.

                    SWANSON
          And I suppose you know this fella?

                    MCKENZIE
          Shit, boy. You're looking at him. I
          got three a' the best coon hounds
          in the territory, trained 'em
          myself. And I know how to track a
          man. Hell, I got nothin' doin' here
          cept fetchin' the Marshal's coffee.
          I bet we could get up there and
          find that bastard and be claimin'
          the reward by week's end. No
          body'll miss me much.

                    SWANSON
          All right, then. Partners, fifty-
          fifty. Let's head out tonight and
          get that bastard.

Swanson puts out his hand, smiling. McKenzie grabs it.

> MCKENZIE
> You must be crazy, boy. Seventy-
> thirty. And I'm not going anywheres
> before I get drunk and get my
> willie wet. We leave at first
> light.

Swanson frowns.

> SWANSON
> Fifty - fifty, or no deal.

> MCKENZIE
> Fine with me. Good luck, then. In
> fact, now that I knows where he is,
> I think I might just go up there
> myself. Hell, I bet I can get that
> bastard single-handed, and then I
> don't have to split that five
> thousand at all.

McKenzie stands and makes to leave.

> SWANSON
> Shit, just wait up now. Dammit,
> okay. You got yourself a partner.

He holds out his hand again to shake.

McKenzie smiles and spits a slimy glob between Swanson's
feet.

> MCKENZIE
> See ya in the mornin', partner.

He turns and swaggers off.

INT. MARKHAM HOUSE - NIGHT

Jacob sits at a bar inside THE MARKHAM HOUSE. He sips whiskey
and plays cards.

Through a doorway in another room, men play various gambling
games and drinking, smoke, and talk loudly.

Various women dressed in revealing clothes with painted faces
move about serving drinks or hanging on men's arms.

A BARTENDER wipes glasses behind the bar.

Jacob, seated alone, pays little attention to others around him.

A Chinese man comes in and approaches the bar. He has a gunny sack heavy with what seems to be small rectangular objects.

The bartender looks up and sees him, then looks at the bag and nods his head towards a door down a short hall.

The Chinese man grunts and looks at the bartender. He motions with his hand in the shape of a glass and makes two quick jerks up to his mouth in the pantomime of someone taking a shot.

The bartender frowns and shakes his head. He jerks his thumb towards the door.

                    BARTENDER
          You know the rules. No drinky till
          after. Now go, they been waitin'.
          Late as usual.

The Chinese man grunts angrily, then stalks through the door.

The bartender shakes his head disgustedly. He calls after him.

                    BARTENDER
          Maybe learn to tell time and speak
          English first for' you 'spect to
          drink at a white man's bar. Damn
          cat-eating savage.

He goes back to wiping glasses as he grumbles under his breath.

Jacob looks up coolly then glances through the door as the Chinese man passes through.

He sees a dark hazy room lit by only candlelight with low couches, men and women stretched out puffing on long pipes.

He looks at the bartender, who is smiling at him, then looks at his drink.

He finishes his glass in one shot and then stacks up his cards.

He puts them in a pocket and gets up and walks calmly toward the door.

The bartender smiles and says as he passes:

> BARTENDER
> Sweet dreams.

Jacob walks through the door.

EXT. BEACH - MORNING

The sun is rising on the beach as gulls start to cry and gather around the piles of refuse strewn about.

On the beach, under a fur blanket, is Sik-way, sleeping. He rouses and sits up, holding his head.

He sees the empty whiskey bottle beside him and picks it up.

He rubs his head and groans. He doubles over and vomits violently.

He sits up and wipes his mouth. He looks at the empty bottle with disgust. He throws it angrily at the seagulls squawking next to him.

> SIK-WAY
> Quiet! Stupid birds.

EXT. SALOON, ALLEY - DAY

Sik-way walks to a rustic wooden door facing the water at the rear of the saloon. He knocks.

A soft commotion is heard inside then, the door opens.

COOKIE, a fat greasy man with a bloody apron steps out, bloody knife in one hand.

He looks at the Sik-way. He grunts.

Sik-way takes out the skin that Tik-wo-tan had given him.

He holds it out.

> SIK-WAY
> (in English)
> Frankie.

Cookie looks at the skin with sharp eyes and reaches his empty hand out to grab it.

Sik-way jerks it back and scowls. He shakes his head no.

> SIK-WAY
> Frankie.

Cookie grunts, sighs, and wipes the bloody knife on his apron.

He jerks his head for Sik-way to follow, then turns and walks inside.

Sik-way follows him to a table in the kitchen where Frankie is eating breakfast.

Tracy stands at a wooden tub scrubbing dishes. One side of her face is cut and bruised.

Frankie looks up at him, stops eating, wipes her mouth.

                    FRANKIE
          Yes?

Sik-way sets the skin down heavily onto the table.

He points at it. He points at his chest.

                    SIK-WAY
               (in English)
          Tik-wo-tan. Make trade.

Frankie sighs and takes the skin and unfolds it carefully, like she's loathe to touch it.

She stares at a large dull gray rock. She turns it over in her hand, then stands and goes to the window, holding it up to the light.

In the light it is slightly translucent and shiny in places.

Sik-way grunts again.

                    SIK-WAY
          Make trade.

                    FRANKIE
          Yes. Yes, we make trade.

Without looking back she points to a large wooden crate on the floor in a corner.

Sik-way bends down quickly and opens it. He smile broadly, showing crooked teeth.

                    SIK-WAY
               (in English)
          Good trade.

Inside the crate, there are a few dozen rifles and boxes of shells.

EXT. WOODS - SUNRISE

McKenzie and Swanson stalk through the woods, led by three
hounds on ropes, sniffing frantically as they go.

Both men carry rifles. Suddenly, the dogs start to bay and
take off at a run. McKenzie, is jerked forward and lets go of
the ropes.

> MCKENZIE
> Shit! They're on a hot scent,
> c'mon'!

They start to run through the trees and thick underbrush
pushing with their rifles in front of them as they go. The
dogs are just ahead, stopped in front of a thick bracket of
thorns, baying and pacing.

The men catch up and stop, breathing hard.

> SWANSON
> Why'd they stop?

> MCKENZIE
> They're spooked. He must be close.
> The bastard must be holed up in
> there.

> SWANSON
> So, what do we do?

McKenzie takes off his hat and wipes his sweating brow. He
looks at Swanson as he takes out a fresh wad of tobacco and
stuffs it in his lip.

He spits.

> MCKENZIE
> We go in and kill that murderin'
> som' bitch.

He checks his rifle and cocks the hammer. He looks at Swanson
and gestures to spread out and flank their prey.

Swanson nods, checks and cocks his rifle, then creeps forward
through the brush bent down low. He goes a ways and stops.

He hears a cracking branch.

He looks around, but sees nothing. Behind him, the dogs are
still whining.

BOOM!

A gunshot rings out and suddenly he hears someone running.

                    MCKENZIE
          I see him! Over here, hurry!

BOOM! BOOM!

More gunshots. Swanson gets up and moves toward the shots.

He stops. He sees McKenzie lying dead on the ground behind a
tree fifteen yards ahead, a single bullet hole between the
eyes.

He quickly ducks behind a tree and crouches down, his back
pressing to the tree.

                    SWANSON
          Shit. Holy Shit.

He looks around frantically, straining to hear a noise. He
hears a faint rustle and realizes it's coming from above him.

He slowly looks straight up, into the tree he is leaning
against.

He freezes and his eyes widen with terror.

                    SWANSON
          Oh, no. NOOOO--

BOOM!

A scream rips the morning air as a gunshot rings out a split
second later, silencing it.

INT. BILL'S CABIN - MORNING

Bill is getting dressed in a small bedroom. On the bed behind
him is LING, a young Chinese woman. She starts to rouse.

Ling looks out the window. Dawn is breaking. She rubs her
eyes then sits up and puts her arms around Bill.

She kisses his neck.

                    LING
          It's too early, come back to bed.

                    BILL
          I have to take our new man up to
          camp this morning and show him the
          ropes. It's going to be a long
          couple of days, for both of us.

He turns and looks at her.

> BILL
> I'll be back in a four or five
> days. You just keep out of sight
> and I'll be back before you know
> it. Just stay here and keep away
> from town.

> LING
> What if you don't come back? What
> if someone finds me here? Please
> Billy, I'm scared. Why can't we
> just leave now?

> BILL
> Hey now, nothing is going to
> happen, you here me? I'm not going
> anywhere darlin' and nobody will
> find you here. As long as you keep
> quiet and stay hidden like we
> talked about.

> LING
> I'm just so scared that he'll find
> me here while you're gone and...

> BILL
> Now, listen. He is not gonna find
> you, you hear me? I will keep you
> safe. And we will leave. Soon.

He kisses her and then stands. He puts on his jacket.

> BILL
> But I told you we can't run away
> empty handed, now can we? Just sit
> tight, darlin', I've got somethin'
> cookin' that'll put us right where
> we need to be. I promise. Now, give
> us a kiss and say goodbye, I'm off.

Bill puts his arms around her and they kiss.

Bill smiles then walks out through the door.

INT. MARKHAM HOUSE - MORNING

Jacob opens his eyes slowly, and sees a naked woman lying on
top of him asleep.

He slowly rolls her off and sits up. He looks around and sees
more naked bodies lying around a few smoldering pipes.

He sits forward and leans on his knees. He's slowly rises and
dresses.

He walks out to the bar where the bartender is wiping glasses
with a filthy rag.

He smiles as Jacob slowly walks out and squints at the
morning sunlight in his eyes, as if his head hurts.

The bartender laughs.

                    BARTENDER
          I see you have a taste for the
          orient, just like your buddy, Mr.
          Hatch.

He smiles. Jacob glares at him. Bill enters through the front
door.

He looks at both men for a moment. The bartender is still
smiling and Jacob looking sleepy and unkempt.

                    BILL
          You're not much of a morning
          person, I think.

                    JACOB
          I was hoping for a cup of coffee.

                    BILL
          No time. We have a long day ahead
          and daylight's a burnin'.

He gestures with his head then turns and leaves. Jacob
follows.

INT. TSE-WHIT-ZEN VILLAGE, LONGHOUSE - DAY

Tik-wo-tan, Siya, Chuk-wa-tal, and other tribal members are
seated in a half circle around a fire in the center of the
longhouse.

Tik-wo-tan stands and looks at the others.

                    TIK-WO-TAN
          Thank you for coming, those who
          have answered my call and left your
          good fishing and hunting grounds.
          These murderers, these Cowichan
          thieves, have struck at us more
          boldly than ever before.
                    (MORE)

70.

                         TIK-WO-TAN (CONT'D)
              They show great disrespect and
              would treat us like the white men
              would treat each other.

There are nods and murmurs as people agree.

                         TIK-WO-TAN
              Now, we have listened to our wise
              elder and sought further guidance
              on this. He has gone to the white
              man village and sought information
              from the Marshal. Siya, what do you
              have to say?

Siya smiles politely, but says nothing. He looks at Chuk-wa-
tal and gestures.

Chuk-wa-tal looks surprised and stands.

He looks around.

                         CHUK-WA-TAL
              The White Marshal had no
              information for us.

He smiles nervously then sits down. Tik-wo-tan looks at him,
satisfied.

                         TIK-WO-TAN
              So, we have found no new evidence
              that this was anything but what it
              seems to be. I think now is the
              time to act. We need to send every
              canoe we have out before the sun
              sets tonight.

He looks around at the other faces, looking for any argument.
There is none.

                         TIK-WO-TAN
              They have my daughter. Your sons.
              They killed our brothers, and they
              have done this to us before. We
              need to show them that we are the
              strong people, and we will not be
              their slaves anymore.

There are many grunts and a few men stand and gather around
Tik-wo-tan.

He starts to sing in a loud ululating cry, hands raised to
the ceiling. Others join in. Soon, a drum is keeping a
steady, deep rhythm.

Chuk-wa-tal watches the crowd, then sees Siya leaving through the door to the rear.

EXT. BEACH - DAY

Siya walks down the beach to the water. Chuk-wa-tal hurries up behind him.

As he approaches, he hears a soft chanting from Siya. He stops after a moment and looks out to the sea.

                    SIYA
          There was a boy named Chuka that I
          sent on a journey to the spirits.
          He came back to me as a man. That
          man carries a spirit with him. A
          spirit that will bring peace to his
          people. His name is Chuk-wa-tal.
          This is his song.

He lifts his head and starts to sing again, louder this time.

Chuk-wa-tal closes his eyes and sways with the rhythm. He opens his eyes and looks down at the crystal on his neck.

It starts to glow and shine with a soft light. He looks at Siya who is singing louder now, arms raised high.

Chuk-wa-tal joins him in the song.

EXT. TRAIL - DAY

Bill and Jacob each lead a pack horse on foot through a winding trail through the woods.

                    JACOB
          So, how far is it to the camp?

                    BILL
          You're not tired already, are you?
          Well, I hope not. I reckon we still
          have five miles solid before we hit
          camp. Best find your legs.

                    JACOB
          It's not the walkin' that's gettin'
          me, it's that I'm walkin' straight
          up a mountain far as I can tell.

Bill chuckles.

72.

                    BILL
          Well, you're right on that count.
          Camp four is seven miles up the
          mountain from Port Crescent to the
          base of Mt. Baldy. That's what I
          call home. I'm camp boss, number
          four is mine. Up above that, at
          Happy Lake, is camp three. Above
          Happy Lake is Sawtooth Ridge.

They walk on in silence for a while. Suddenly, a commotion is
heard ahead and they stop to see what it is.

Louis Blair comes running down the trail at full speed, then
stops in front of them, breathing heavily.

                    BILL
          Where the blazes are you coming
          from in such a hurry?

                    BLAIR
          High camp. Swanson left to get the
          Marshal two days ago and never came
          back. This mornin', we hear
          gunshots from up at Sawtooth Ridge.
          So a few boys head up there and
          found Swanson and the Marshal's
          deputy shot dead, both of em. One
          neat hole drilled right between the
          eyes for each. The bodies were laid
          in a shallow grave, no effort to
          hide them was taken. They was laid
          out in a "T".

                    JACOB
          Jesus.

                    BILL
          Why'd Swanson go to get the
          Marshal? And, if he did, where is
          the Marshal?

                    BLAIR
          That's on account of Emil. He's a
          big krout fella, sturdy som' bitch.
          Well, he seen somethin' scared him
          clean to the bone. Burst into camp
          and got his stuff, skinned right
          out that night! Scared all us
          stiff, what with the talk of the
          wild man bein' nearby and all.
                    (MORE)

                    BLAIR (CONT'D)
          So, Swanson says to relax and he'd
          go see the Marshal and settle the
          business. 'Cept he don't come back,
          then we hear those shots.

                    JACOB
          Just exactly who, or what is this
          wild man?

                    BLAIR
          Damn boy, you never hear tell of
          the wild man o' the Olympics, John
          Turnow? Shoot, you must be the only
          dude in the territory.

                    BILL
          He's just a man. A man who likes
          trees and squirrels more than
          people and last spring decides to
          kill his two darling twin nephews
          and abscond himself from the
          company of men permanently.

                    BLAIR
          That ain't the half of it. They say
          he's more ape than man. He swings
          through the trees and can vanish
          and re-appear like a demon.

                    BILL
          Sure, and he shoots white lightning
          from his arse.

                    BLAIR
          Anyways, I'm off to round up some
          boys and fresh hounds and get that
          freak. The bodies were laid down at
          the bottom of a steep knoll like
          he's taunting us. I think he's
          holed up there and now's the time
          to go in heavy and take him. It
          ain't about the five thousand
          anymore. This mother's campin' in
          our backyard and we need to clean
          house.

                    JACOB
          Five thousand?

                    BILL
          Dollars laddy. That's the price on
          Turnow's head.

Jacob looks interested now. Blair wipes his brow, then nods.

                    BLAIR
          Well, I best be going, no time to
          kill. If you boys want to join in,
          you know where to go. I'll be back
          and headed up before dark, and
          tonight we'll be drinking to that
          beast's cold carcass.

Blair runs off again, headed down the trail.

INT. SALOON - DAY

In a small back room of the saloon, Frankie sits at a small
wooden desk, writing on an envelope. She finishes writing,
then drops a large stone inside.

She seals it with a glob of wax, then places it in a large
safe that is behind the desk.

The shelves in the safe are filled with similar envelopes.

She closes the safe. The door has a painting of Niagara Falls
on it, which now hides the safe from view.

Behind her a prostitute, SALLY, knocks on the door frame.

Frankie turns and looks at her, then smiles. She smooths down
the back of her dress then sits down.

                    FRANKIE
          Sally, come on in, hon'.

Sally steps in. There are no other seats in the room. She
looks at her feet and says nothing.

                    FRANKIE
          What's on your mind, girl?

                    SALLY
          Well, Frankie, I wanted to ask you
          a favor.

                    FRANKIE
          Okay. Go ahead, then.

                    SALLY
          Well, it's just... It makes me so
          mad, every time a john takes a
          liking to me that bitch Eva is all
          over him! Seducing him and his coin
          into her filthy bed. Just cause'
          I'm youngest too, I know it.
                    (MORE)

                    SALLY (CONT'D)
          That bitch has always had it out
          for me, I swear it.

                    FRANKIE
          I see. And it happened again?

                    SALLY
          Oh, it's been happening for a long
          time, and yeah, it happened again.
          For the last time, Frankie, I swear
          it.

Sally flushes with anger and her eyes flash. Frankie smiles.

She stands and walks around the desk to Sally.

She looks at her for a moment then smiles warmly.

She takes her hands gently.

                    FRANKIE
          I'm sorry, sweetie, I really am. I
          do know how the girls can be,
          especially to someone so young and
          pretty as you. Shoot, it's no
          wonder Eva is jealous, just look at
          you girl--

She steps back and looks Sally up and down.

                    FRANKIE
          Perfect figure, full red lips,
          silken blonde tresses. I think I'd
          be mighty jealous too, if I had to
          compete against a creature like you
          for a man's attention.

Sally flushes then smiles, flattered.

                    FRANKIE
          Tell you what? Why don't you just
          keep doing what you do best, be
          your gorgeous self, and I'll go and
          have a little talk with Eva.

Sally smiles and hugs Frankie. Behind them, sounds of someone
approaching.

Frankie looks over Sally's shoulder and sees a short stocky
man, BUSTER KELLY, walking toward them.

She pulls herself away from Sally. Sally turns and sees Kelly
then nods at Frankie and leaves.

Frankie nods back then walks back behind her desk and sits as
Kelly strolls in.

She looks up at him and he smiles back, taking off his hat.

                    KELLY
          Morning, ma'am. A schooner just
          made port, six men overboard. I
          have my man bringing them here for
          rooms as we speak.

                    FRANKIE
          I see. And I suppose you want these
          men to check all valuables in right
          away once they get here?

                    KELLY
          Of course. You can accommodate
          them, I assume?

                    FRANKIE
          Of course. But I'm afraid after
          that last unfortunate incident we
          need to renegotiate our terms.

                    KELLY
          And you think I'm at fault for
          that? Even though it was my men who
          suffered?

                    FRANKIE
          And how would that be my fault? I
          did what I promised. You can't
          blame me for your men not doing
          their job.

                    KELLY
          Well, that's the problem. That dude
          wasn't doped enough, and he woke up
          and caused hell when he shoulda'
          been sleeping like a baby. You are
          to blame for that, beggin' your
          pardon of course, ma'am.

                    FRANKIE
          Oh, of course. Well, now I guess we
          just don't see things eye to eye.
          You should take your business
          elsewhere, mayhaps.

Kelly's face darkens and he fidgets with his hat.

                    KELLY
          Now, Frankie, I didn't mean
          offense. I just don't think--

                    FRANKIE
          Now, you listen. I don't want to
          know what you think, Buster Kelly.
          I don't trust you any farther than
          I can spit. And since your men
          don't seem up to handling a little
          trouble, I think the price of doing
          business has just gone up for you,
          my friend. I want thirty dollars a
          head now, no exceptions. And I want
          first pick, every time. I know you
          play me against Liz across the
          street at the Globe. I'm not
          greedy, I know you need to work
          with us both. But, from now on, I
          get exclusive pick to every man who
          steps on the dock. Agreed?

Kelly frowns and stares at her. She smiles back, waiting.

Men come through the front door and start to shuffle toward
them. Six sailors led by Kelly's man.

Frankie eyes them as they approach. They are only seconds
away.

                    FRANKIE
          Well, what do you say, Buster? Do
          we have a deal, or should I take
          things on my own from here?

She holds out here hand to shake. He looks at it. Right
before the men get to them he grabs it tightly.

She smiles a huge welcoming smile.

                    FRANKIE
          Welcome to the Olympian House,
          gentlemen. We're going to tend to
          your every need, don't you worry.
          Miss Frankie is going to take good
          care of you now.

EXT. LOGGING CAMP - DAY

Jacob follows behind Bill as they emerge out of a mountain
trail.

They walk into a small clearing in the trees where a small
cluster of wooden, shack-like buildings are grouped closely
together.

A man is chopping firewood to the side of the largest
building.

Smoke curls from a metal stovepipe jutting out of the rough,
split-shake roof.

Bill ties up his pack horse to the hitching post in front of
the main building, which is a long mess hall and kitchen.

Jacob does the same. He looks around and takes in the
surroundings.

Bill claps him on the shoulder.

> BILL
> C'mon, let's have a quick bite
> before we head out to the fall
> site. We'll catch up with the boys
> and finish out the day.

They walk inside.

INT. MESS HALL - DAY

They sit, eating a rustic ham sandwich. Sounds are heard
outside and they look up.

Two men come in through the door breathing hard. Blair and
another man, JIM ELDRED.

They start to grab biscuits and slices of ham and wrap them
in napkins, tucking them away inside of pockets.

Blair looks back at Bill.

> BLAIR
> We're headed up. Just fillin' water
> skins and grabin' a few provisions
> in case we have to hold over
> through the night.

Bill grunts and nods and Blair goes back to his task.

> JACOB
> I thought you would have more men.
> It just the two of you?

Blair grunts, and shakes his head, putting the last napkins
in pockets now full.

                    BLAIR
          You and me both, friend. But, all
          crews are workin' today and no one
          around seems willing risk his neck
          up there after Swanson and that
          deputy were killed. Hell, I can't
          says that I blame em'. Most these
          boys are just workin' stiffs. We
          just ain't got any real gunmen
          'round here. These boys ain't here
          to get shot up by some crazy man,
          no matter how big the reward.

Jacob looks at Bill and Bill looks back. Blair turns to
Eldred.

                    BLAIR
          It's time, boys. Wish us luck now.

He grabs the rifle he'd set down on a table and nods at Jacob
and Bill.

Jacob stands.

                    JACOB
          Wait.

He looks at Bill. Bill looks at him for a moment then smiles
and chuckles softly.

                    BILL
          Go on then, you daft bastard.

                    JACOB
          I'll see you soon.

He picks up his hat and jacket and follows the two men out
the door.

EXT. TSE-WHIT-ZEN VILLAGE - DUSK

Twenty-five or more canoes sit on the beach in front of the
village. The whole tribe helps to load the canoes with
supplies.

Songs are being sung as women and men work together and
prepare for battle.

To one side, Tik-wo-tan is loading up a canoe with long
spears tipped with curving whale bone points.

Sik-way loads the neighboring canoe.

Tik-wo-tan comes over and stand beside him. He looks at a
pile of rifles gleaming in the fading light. Tik-wo-tan nods
and pats Sik-way on the back.

                    TIK-WO-TAN
          You did well. You will be rewarded
          for your bravery and for your
          victory in battle.

                    SIK-WAY
          Will you tell the people before we
          go, or am I to keep it secret among
          a chosen few? We have enough rifles
          to arm a third of the men at least.

                    TIK-WO-TAN
          I will wait to tell. Only give the
          rifles to the men you trust to keep
          it secret until you attack. Once it
          is done, I will openly share our
          plans with the people. When we are
          celebrating our greatest victory
          yet, they can hardly disagree with
          our methods. The world is changed
          now and many are too foolish to see
          it. But, I will not let our people
          be washed away by the stinking tide
          of the white man. We will show them
          that we are the Klallam. We are the
          Strong People, and this is our
          home.

                    SIK-WAY
          I will bring back your daughter and
          I will honor our fathers with the
          blood of our enemies. They will
          fear the Strong People after
          tonight, I promise you.

                    TIK-WO-TAN
          I know you will. Now, let's join
          our people in one last song. It's
          time to launch.

They walk to the center of the crowd and Tik-wo-tan lifts his
arms and speaks loudly so all can hear.

                    TIK-WO-TAN
          Join me now, as we sing the song of
          the Strong People and prepare to
          send our brave warriors off, to
          restore honor to our name and
          return our sons and daughters. Let
          us sing a blessing to protect them.
                    (MORE)

                    TIK-WO-TAN (CONT'D)
          To give them the strength of the
          elk, the cunning of the fox, the
          speed of the eagle, and to take the
          spirits of our people with them, so
          our enemies can see the faces of
          our people as they die, and know
          that they have done this to
          themselves.

He lifts his voice in a loud song and many voices join in.

Drums are soon beating the steady rhythm and the sound
carries across the still water toward the setting sun.

INT. SALOON - NIGHT

Kelly sits in a dark corner of the saloon at a table with two
other men: Gundersen, now with an eye-patch, and Black Pete,
now with a rough leather patch where his nose should be.

                    GUNDERSEN
          So, I heard tell over at the Globe
          that your miss Frankie did a little
          trade with that Indian fellow who
          was in town yesterday. No one seem
          to know what she traded for, but
          she had one of Levi's men get her a
          full crate of rifles and ammo.
          Quite a little stash hear tell.

                    KELLY
          That bitch is set on running this
          town, it seems. That just ain't
          gonna' happen boys. It's time we
          made a move of our own. What we
          need is a place of our own. Our own
          boarding house. Then I can deal
          with Frankie right, once and for
          all.

                    PETE
          We need to get into that damn safe.
          She has a fortune in there, I hear.
          They say a fortune in stones.

                    KELLY
          Stones?

Pete smiles a horrible nose-less smile showing large gold
teeth.

                    PETE
          Precious stones.

EXT. WOODS - DAWN

Jacob, Blair, and Eldred huddle behind a group of small shrubs.

They look tired, exhausted. Steam from their sweaty bodies glows in the cold morning air.

Jacob looks at Blair. Then Eldred. Jacob nods.

> BLAIR
> *(in a hushed voice)*
> He's got to be up in the thicket
> ahead somewhere. It dead ends on a
> shear drop off. There's nowhere
> else to go.

> JACOB
> Okay, let's spread out and make a
> final push through. Stay far apart
> as you can without losing eyeline
> of the man closest to you. I'll
> take the middle, you two take the
> flanks. Go slow and quiet. Let's
> finish this now.

The two men nod, then they move out. Jacob stalks straight forward slowly and keeps his eyes on both men.

They creep forward for a few long moments. Jacob hears something moving ahead and looks around slowly.

Suddenly, Jacob sees quick movement on his right and Blair falls to his knees and draws up his rifle to fire.

BOOM!

There is a deafening shot before he can get his rifle all the way up.

Blair's head jerks back in an explosion of blood as he falls backwards.

Jacob rushes in as he hears Eldred open fire. Shots ring out!

Jacob strains to see and then spots gun smoke from ahead, rising from behind a bush.

He pulls his rifle and waits until he sees the smoke from another shot again, then opens fire.

He empties his rifle and ducks behind a tree. He pants, breathing heavy, then swallows and forces his breathing to slow.

He waits. Silence. No shots, no movement.

He slowly creeps back the way they came in.

EXT. LOGGING CAMP - DAY

Jacob walks into the camp to find a large group of men and several teams of hounds.

All the men are armed. As he comes into camp, Marshal pushes through the crowd that has turned to look at him and runs forward to meet him.

Bill comes up behind Marshal. They look at Jacob.

> MARSHAL
> They heard shots at dawn and some
> men ran to town to fetch me. After
> what happened to McKenzie... Well,
> I rounded up every man handy and
> here I am. We were just about to
> head up the ridge.

> JACOB
> Good. Let's go. I'm not certain,
> but I believe your wild man is
> dead. At the least, he's wounded
> and not moving.

> MARSHAL
> What about Blair and Eldred?

> JACOB
> Not positive about Eldred, but
> Blair is dead. I have a feeling
> that, if Eldred was still alive,
> we'd have seen him by now. I waited
> a good three hours before I moved,
> and didn't hear anything stirring
> up there at all. All the same, I
> figured I'd get backup before I
> went in to fetch him. Either he's
> dead or he's dying, so no sense in
> taking chances now.

> MARSHAL
> You did good, son. Mr. Miller is
> it? I've heard rumors of your
> recent exploits in town. Seems you
> are set on making quite an
> impression here.

They stare at each other. Marshal grins. He turns to the group.

> MARSHAL
> All right, boys, we're moving out!

They turn and head up the hill, two dozen men and hounds following.

EXT. WOODS - SUNSET

Jacob and Marshal stand over the body of Eldred, who is laying crumpled on his knees, head backwards awkwardly.

His gun is laying across his arms and he has a single bullet hole between the eyes, a dried line of blood running down one side of his head.

A voice calls out from fifty yards away.

> MAN
> Marshal! Over here!

Jacob and Marshal approach three men huddled over a body and they step away as they come near.

Lying on the ground is a large man with a long shaggy beard and wild unkempt hair, full of pine needles and twigs.

A rifle lays next to him and he has a ragged cloak on seemingly hand stitched together from many different furs.

Marshal leans in. He looks the man over and then straightens up.

He turns to Jacob. He puts out his hand.

> MARSHAL
> Fine work, son. You did well here
> today.

Jacob looks at him slightly flushed for a second, then takes his hand.

> MARSHAL
> Now, let's get back to town so you
> can claim that reward and I can get
> the body ready to ship to Olympia.

> JACOB
> I'll claim no more than one third,
> the other two thirds should go to
> the families of Blair and Eldred.

Marshal nods. They turn and Marshal watches as Jacob walks
ahead.

INT. SALOON - NIGHT

Black Pete sits with a girl. They drink at the bar.

A man is playing a fiddle on the stage and a few drunk men
dance with girls on the floor.

Two men come in excited and talking loudly. The music stops
and everyone looks at them.

                    MAN 1
          They got him, boys! The wild man is
          dead!

                    MAN 2
          He killed two men, but that cowboy
          that went up with them killed the
          son of a bitch.

Black Pete stands quickly and comes over to the two of them.

People clear a path as he comes.

The first man looks at Pete with wide eyes as he approaches.

                    MAN 1
          Holy hell.

Pete strides up and stand before him.

                    PETE
          What cowboy?

                    MAN 2
          What in the name of sweet Christ
          happened to you?

Pete looks at the second man, then quickly pulls a knife out
and stabs him in the neck.

Blood gushes and he gargles a scream.

Pete grabs the other man and puts the knife to his throat.

                    PETE
          Was his name Miller?

                    MAN 1
          I, I'm not sure. I think so.

                    PETE
          Where?

                    MAN 1
          Port Crescent. They got him up
          above the logging camp, they're
          bringing him down now. We just got
          the news and... please.

Pete growls then lets go of the man. He drops his knife. It
sticks into the wood plank floor.

The man whimpers. He looks at his dead friend then starts to
babble.

                    MAN 1
          Oh god, oh my god! You killed him!

Pete smiles a hideous gold-toothed smile then reaches forward
with both hands, grabs the man's head and gives it a violent
twist. His neck breaks and he falls dead.

Pete looks up to find Frankie glaring at him from behind the
bar.

Pete takes out a single coin, flips it on the floor between
the two men he just killed, and winks at Frankie.

                    PETE
          For the mess.

He smiles wider and walks out of the saloon.

EXT. BEACH - NIGHT

A group of cedar dug-out canoes glide silently to a black
shoreline lit only by moonlight.

They pull up on the beach and men begin to line up and face a
small group of wooden houses just up the beach.

A group of men gather by a canoe at the end. Sik-way silently
hands them rifles.

Sik-way looks at them and nods. He walks to the front of the
main group.

Murmurs pass through the group as they eye the new rifles
gleaming in the moonlight.

He turns to the group, confusion on the face of some. He
speaks in a loud whisper.

                    SIK-WAY
          Brothers, tonight we become strong
          once again. Get our people back,
          and take any captives you can for
          yourselves. We are the strong
          people. We will fear no one.

He turns and motions for the others to follow. They crouch
and silently stalk up the beach.

They get to the edge of the grass and suddenly dogs start to
growl and run at them, barking.

A man stands with a spear ready to throw at the dog, but
before he can Sik-way opens fire with his rifle and the dog
falls in a bloody pile.

All at once, there is chaos as people start to stream from
the longhouses.

Sik-way opens fire as people rush out. The defenseless people
die within seconds.

Bodies quickly litter the grass. Everywhere, there is
screaming.

More men with rifles join in. Soon, the air is filled with
gun smoke and the wailing cries of the hurt and dying.

It's a massacre.

EXT. PORT ANGELES - DAY

A group of men stand in front of The Olympian House. They
gather around a coffin which is propped up against a wall on
the porch of the saloon.

A man, TIMOTHY CAINE, approaches on horseback and hitches in
front of the crowd.

With him, THE CAMERA MAN, dismounts and begins unloading a
large wooden camera.

Caine pulls a leather bound journal from his saddle bags. He
joins the crowd and addresses a man, LEROY, who is standing
next to him.

                    CAINE
          Good morning. I'm Thomas Caine from
          the Seattle Post. I'm here to do a
          story on the capture of John
          Turnow, the so-called Wild Man of
          the Olympics. That must be him?

                    LEROY
          Nice to meet you Mr. Caine. Name's
          Leroy, Frank Leroy. That's him all
          right.

                    CAINE
          So, word is the Marshal got him
          with a posse two nights ago, but
          another man shot him. You know who
          that man is?

                    LEROY
          Sorry, can't say I do. All I know
          is he's some dude from down south,
          a real cowboy type.

                    CAINE
          He's not from around here? Not one
          of the loggers from the camp?

                    LEROY
          Hell, nobody's from around here.
          But, he ain't been around long, if
          that's what you mean. He'll be here
          with the Marshal any minute. They's
          supposed to open up the casket so's
          we can all get a good look at the
          devil. I hear tell he's more ape
          than man, seven foot tall with
          hands bigger than dinner plates.

                    CAINE
          I see. Thank you, Mr. Leroy.

Jacob and Marshal walk out of the saloon and step onto the
porch, clearing men back.

As they come out Jacob sees Kelly, Pete, and Gundersen
standing across the street, watching him.

He stops for a second and stares back. Kelly smiles and tips
his hat.

Jacob nods at them.

                    MARSHAL
          All right, all right. Now, listen.
          I will open the casket for pictures
          so everyone can get a proper look
          at the monster that you've all been
          so excited about this last year.
                    (MORE)

                    MARSHAL (CONT'D)
          You can all rest easy to know he's
          no more than an ordinary man, just
          like you and me, and that he will
          terrorize your thoughts no more.

He nods at a man with a pry bar and he removes the lid.

Everyone mutters and pushes closer.

The camera man, who has set up a large camera on a wooden
tripod, snaps a picture with a flash and a cloud of smoke.

People pose in front of the body and more pictures are taken.

A man leans in before the picture is taken and cuts a slice
from the corpse's jacket.

He holds it up for the picture and people cheer in approval.

Others do the same.

INT. SALOON - DAY

Jacob and Marshal now watch the commotion through the
windows.

                    MARSHAL
          You seem to handle yourself well,
          Jacob. You know, since McKenzie is
          gone, I need a new deputy, and I
          could use a man like yourself.

Jacob stares out the window as more pictures flash. He
doesn't respond.

                    MARSHAL
          I know you were planning on
          starting up at Lehman's operation.
          I talked to the camp boss, Hatch.
          He says you were a lawman before
          and that you'd be better off here
          anyways than stuck up in some
          logging camp. Hell, it was his idea
          for me to offer.

Jacob looks at him.

                    MARSHAL
          But, I wouldn't offer if I didn't
          think he was right. So, what do you
          say?

Jacob sighs and turns to stare out the window again.

                         JACOB
               Thanks, Marshal, that is
               appreciated. I was a lawman, true.
               Or, at least, I thought I was,
               but...

Just then loud frenzied footsteps are heard from the porch
and voices were speaking sharply.

They could see shuffling and pushing around the coffin.

EXT. PORT ANGELES - DAY

Men are pushing in at the coffin while another man is trying
with little success to push them back.

Jacob is shocked to see that they have stripped the body of
clothes and are cutting away pieces of flesh now for
souvenirs: fingers, ears, pieces of skin.

He bursts in and draws his gun, firing twice in the air to
clear the crowd.

Silence falls and all eyes look at him. He grabs the lid and
slams it back on the coffin.

The Marshal runs up and draws his pistol.

                         MARSHAL
               All right, that's enough. Show's
               over, everyone. Disperse or the
               next man to step forward will spend
               the night in jail for disturbing
               the peace. What's it gonna be?

He looks around as everyone shrinks back and starts to
disappear down streets and into doors.

Jacob and Marshal holster their guns and watch the crowd go.

Caine comes to them.

                         CAINE
               Marshal, I'm Timothy Caine from the
               Seattle Post. I was wondering if I
               could get an interview about the
               events that led up to Turnow's
               capture. I understand four men were
               killed?

Jacob shrinks back at hearing this and starts to retreat.

                    CAINE
              (calling to Jacob)
          Excuse me, sir, but I believe you
          were the one who actually shot
          Turnow, isn't that right? I'd love
          to hear your account firsthand, of
          course. I'm sure the whole
          territory does.

                    JACOB
          Sorry, not interested. I'm sure the
          Marshal can tell you everything
          that matters. And, I'd appreciate
          it if my name weren't mentioned at
          all. I'm not looking for any
          credit.

                    CAINE
          Well, I at least need to publish
          your name, for the sake of
          journalistic integrity. People
          deserve to know the truth, sir. The
          whole truth.

                    JACOB
          I agree. But I don't talk to
          reporters and I don't want my name
          published.

He stares at Caine for a moment before nodding at Marshal and
leaving.

Caine shakes his head.

                    CAINE
          Marshal, surely you know this
          information is the public's right,
          and trying to keep it secret isn't
          only morally wrong, but foolish.

                    MARSHAL
          I will respect the man's wishes and
          ask that you do the same. Now, you
          want that interview? After you.

He opens the saloon door and they go inside.

INT. SALOON, FRANKIE'S OFFICE - DAY

Frankie is in her office.

She turns, opens her safe, and removes a stone wrapped in a
skin. She sets it on the table.

Tracy walks in with another man, ALBERT STIEN.

                    TRACY
          Frankie, a man is here to see you.

Tracy eyes the safe with the door slightly open. From where
she stands, she can see in a crack, and she notices a small
prayer book lying near the front edge of a shelf.

                    STIEN
          Madame Frankie, I'm Albert Stien
          from Stien & Sons Jewelry in
          Tacoma. I got your telegram and
          came right away. It took some days
          to get here. I normally wouldn't
          consider making such a trip,
          especially at short notice, but...
          Well, this was something I had to
          see right away.

                    FRANKIE
          Welcome, Mr. Stien. Have a seat. I
          do thank you for making the long
          trip out, and I can assure you it
          wasn't a waste of your time.

She looks at Tracy and gestures with her head. Tracy nods
then leaves, closing the door behind her.

INT. SALOON - DAY

Tracy closes the door and walks out to the bar. Caine sits at
the bar, drinking whiskey.

He's writing in his journal furiously. He finishes then
closes it with a grunt.

He sighs and finishes his whiskey. He sees Tracy and smiles.

                    CAINE
          Say, miss, I was wondering if you
          can help me.

                    TRACY
          I suppose I might. What is it?

                    CAINE
          It seems the hero of my story
          doesn't want his name published,
          and the Marshal is protecting him
          for some reason. I have all the
          goods, just not the name of the man
          who actually brought Turnow down.
                    (MORE)

> CAINE (CONT'D)
> I have to get this story in right
> away. I just need that name and no
> one seems to know or won't say.

Tracy smiles. Caine removes two gold coins. He holds them out.

Tracy holds out her hand and he drops the coins in.

> TRACY
> Miller. Jacob Miller.

She tucks the coins in her cleavage and winks. He scribbles the name and then grabs his coat and hurries to the door.

EXT. LIGHTHOUSE - DAY

A man, GEORGE SMITH, is standing in front of a lighthouse on a beach overlooking the bay.

He is chopping firewood and stacking it against the side of the light house.

He stops and looks up. Coming down the beach just a few yards away is a native woman, WAH-SUB.

She is bleeding from her side and staggering. She is pregnant.

In her hand is a slender whale bone club, elaborately carved.

She falls to the sand in front of him. Smith drops the axe and runs to her.

> SMITH
> Oh my god! Come here, let me help
> you.

He picks the women up and she gets shakily to her feet.

Tears are streaming down her cheeks and she looks at him.

INT. LIGHTHOUSE - DAY

Smith helps Wah-sub down on a couch.

He gently lifts up her shirt to reveal a bullet wound just above her belly below her left breast.

She moans in pain an grabs her pregnant stomach.

94.

                    SMITH
          Who did this to you? Are you from
          the village around the point?

                    WAH-SUB
          Sik-way. Tse-whit-zen.

                    SMITH
          What's that? I don't understand.
          Don't worry, now. I'll go and fetch
          the doctor. You're safe now.

He pats her head gently then smiles. She holds up the club
and offers it to him. He takes it and tucks it in his jacket

                    SMITH
          I guess I best fetch the constable
          and see if we can get this business
          sorted out too now while I'm at it.
          Just sit tight, I'll be back with
          help.

He gets her a glass of water and she smiles weakly and
drinks, then coughs and starts to moan again and grasp at her
belly.

EXT. TSE-WHIT-ZEN VILLAGE - SUNSET

Everyone stands on the beach in front of the village as a
group of canoes comes ashore.

Sik-way is in the lead canoe. As he comes in, he lets out a
cry and raises a slender whale bone club in his hand.

The other canoes behind him join his cry and the people on
the beach begin to sing a joyful song and beat drums.

Men pull rifles from canoes and fire them in the air with
cries of joy.

Captives with hands and feet tied with rope are led from the
canoes. The captives are seated in a row on the beach.

Tik-wo-tan comes down to greet Sik-way, who is leading three
young girls up the beach.

                    SIK-WAY
          For you, my chief. Take these
          captives as a sign of my honor and
          respect for you. We had a great
          victory and it was because of you.

He hands Tik-wo-tan the rope leading the girls. He takes it
and smiles, but looks at the beach expectantly.

                    TIK-WO-TAN
          And what of the princess and the
          others? What of our people?

                    SIK-WAY
          She wasn't there. They didn't have
          any captives.

Tik-wo-tan looks away toward the longhouse. Siya and Chuk-wa-
tal stand in front of the large totem pole that guards the
entrance.

Siya turns and walks back inside. Chuk-wa-tal returns his
gaze.

                    SIK-WAY
          This was a good victory for us. The
          spirits were on our side. We struck
          our enemy down, and now they will
          fear us. This was a good day.

                    TIK-WO-TAN
          You did good, Sik-way. Here, keep
          them, you earned them. They will
          serve you well or bring you wealth.

He hands Sik-way the rope back. Sik-way beams proudly and
nods slightly. He walks up the beach to a wooden hut.

Tik-wo-tan watches as elaborately carved wooden masks are put
on and skin and feathered capes are donned. A celebration is
underway.

People start to move in a rhythmic group as more costumed
dancers join in.

More rifles are fired as people pass them around and try them
out.

They sing and dance with the sun setting behind them, the sky
ablaze.

EXT. BILL'S CABIN - NIGHT

Bill approaches his small cabin in the woods. He has a lit
lantern and is leading a pack horse behind him.

He stops in front of the cabin and looks around. It's dark
inside and the wood stovepipe isn't spewing smoke, even
though it's a clear, cold night.

He approaches slowly and goes to the door. It's ajar.

INT. BILL'S CABIN - NIGHT

He rushes in and finds everything strewn about and furniture overturned.

He goes to the small bedroom at the back and puts his lantern in front of him.

Ling is lying naked on the bed with her hands and feet tied.

Her neck is cut.

Blood is everywhere and she is dead. Bill looks for a moment then backs out slowly. He screams in the night.

> BILL
> NOOOO!

EXT. SLOOP - MORNING

Kelly, Gundersen, and Pete sit on a small sloop anchored off shore.

They are drinking ale and eating a loaf of hard bread. Kelly stares at the Olympian House, which is in front of them in the center of the small town.

Gundersen stands and walks to the rail beside Kelly. He burps then begins to pee over the railing into the water. He looks at Kelly and grins.

> GUNDERSEN
> Let's just go in and take the
> bitch. She has no real muscle. She
> needs to pay.

Kelly continues to stare at the building.

> GUNDERSEN
> I say, go in now and take care of
> her once and for all.

Pete stands and comes behind them.

> PETE
> I'm ready. I need to kill that
> cowboy. He's in there, I know it.

Kelly spits and lights a cigar. He still stares at the building.

                    KELLY
          Oh, she's going to pay. The dude
          too. But, we can't be stupid
          either. Look at us eating this
          stale loaf. We should be the ones
          in there. It's time we made our
          move boys. This town is up for the
          taking, and I'll be damned if I let
          some red-headed whore be the one to
          take it.

                    GUNDERSEN
          So, what's the plan?

                    KELLY
          We wait until late. Then, tonight
          we go in. I'll set a fire in the
          kitchen to distract everyone, then
          you and Petey will blow the safe
          and get the loot. No one will know
          who did it in all the confusion.
          We'll have all her money, and her
          place will burn. And in all the
          confusion, who knows who might just
          die mysteriously.

Pete and Gundersen grin evilly.

INT. CUSTOMS HOUSE - DAY

LT. MERRYMAN, sits in a cozy office behind a desk. He wears
naval uniform and smokes a brier pipe.

Smith comes in through the door and stands before him.

                    MERRYMAN
          Mr. Smith, please have a seat. So,
          you found this woman near the
          lighthouse, is that right?

                    SMITH
          Yes, sir. She walked up like a
          ghost while I was chopping
          firewood. She doesn't speak a word
          of English so I have no idea what
          she was trying to tell me. All I
          know is she kept saying Tse-whit-
          zen. And she had this.

He takes out the whale bone club. Merryman takes it and looks
at it. He looks up at Smith.

> MERRYMAN
> Well Mr. Smith, this does shed some
> light on things. Tse-whit-zen is
> the indian village across the
> straight near Port Angeles. They've
> been enemies of the local tribe
> here on Vancouver Island, the
> Cowichan, for centuries. The woman
> is Cowichan. We went to the village
> yesterday after reports of an
> exceptionally brutal raid. It was
> wiped out. Everyone massacred. And
> this...

He holds up the slender club.

> MERRYMAN
> ... this is a club they use on
> raids, called a slave killer. A
> nasty piece of work designed for
> crushing a skull with one blow and
> delivering a silent death. This
> particular one has the markings of
> the Klallam on it. An attacker must
> have dropped it in the violence.
> But, it seems these attackers, at
> least some, used high caliber
> rifles as well. The village was
> defenseless.

> SMITH
> Oh my God. What savages! What are
> you going to do?

> MERRYMAN
> I'm going to find these murderers.
> And I'm going to make sure that
> they pay for their crimes.

INT. LAUNDRY HOUSE - DAY

A Chinese man, HAN, works over a steaming pile of laundry.

Bill bursts through the door, dirty and blood all over his
hands and clothes.

Han looks up startled and drops his work. He runs for the
back door.

Bill chases him and tackles him by the back door. He beats
him savagely, until he is still.

INT. SALOON - NIGHT

The saloon of the Olympian House is crowded. A group of men playing lively music on the small stage.

Jacob plays cards by himself at a small table. Tracy sees him and comes over.

He sees her and nods. She sits down. He looks at her bruised face, almost healed now.

He sighs and downs his whiskey.

>   JACOB
> You look thirsty. Can I buy you a
> whiskey?

Tracy smiles seductively and gets up. She walks around to him and leans over his shoulder and speaks softly in his ear.

>   TRACY
> Hon, I thought you'd never ask.
> Allow me. I'll be right back.

She walks to the bar and returns with a bottle and a glass for herself.

She pours him a fresh one then one for herself. She holds the glass up for a toast.

He looks at her and meets her gaze. They softly touch glasses.

INT. SALOON, BEDROOM - NIGHT

Jacob and Tracy are now in a room upstairs, kissing. Tracy unbuttons his shirt and he sits on the bed.

She pulls his shirt off slowly. She runs her hands down his chest.

She pulls her hair forward and turns her back to him. He reaches out and unties her corset.

She turns and meets him, their bare chests heaving with heavy breath and they kiss.

They fall onto the bed and make love.

INT. SALOON - NIGHT

Tracy moves silently through the saloon in the blackness of the night.

She is dressed in only a nightgown. She moves into Frankie's office and over to the large safe.

She slowly turns the handle and does the combination. She opens it with a click.

She reaches in and pulls out a small payer book. She opens it and takes out a small pistol concealed inside.

She puts the book back. She pulls out her hand but it touches something large.

She pulls it out. It's the stone. She unwraps it and looks at it.

She hears a noise from outside and she quickly closes the safe.

EXT. SALOON - NIGHT

Kelly is standing out back of the saloon with a torch blazing and a handkerchief over his face.

He tosses the torch through the back window of the kitchen then runs off into the night.

INT. SALOON, BEDROOM - NIGHT

CRASH!

Jacob wakes up and Tracy is there sitting up in bed beside him, already awake.

>   JACOB
>   What was that?

He gets up and goes to the window. He can see a faint glow like a fire burning.

Suddenly, commotion is heard and someone screams. Jacob gets his boots and clothes on quickly and helps Tracy.

INT. SALOON - NIGHT

They rush down the hall banging on doors.

                    JACOB
          Fire, Fire, everyone up and move!
          Now! Fire!

As they start down the stairs, a huge explosion rocks the
building.

Tracy falls and Jacob helps her up.

CRASH!

The giant deer antler chandelier falls to the floor with a
crash.

Screaming continues. Jacob helps people down the stairs and
out the front door.

The fire grows in the kitchen.

Jacob leaves Tracy to help the last of the people down the
stairs.

The fire now engulfs the entire kitchen. Pots and pans crash
down as the roof collapses.

Jacob hears coughing and sees a shape in the haze, huddled
behind the bar.

He rushes over. Frankie sits covered in blood from a gash in
her head. She coughs violently. The smoke is getting thicker
by the second.

Jacob helps Frankie up and pulls her out from behind the bar.
Tracy helps him bring her outside.

EXT. PORT ANGELES - NIGHT

Men rush with buckets filled with water from the beach and
forming a line to pass it from the water to the fire in an
unbroken line of hands.

Frankie, Tracy, and Jacob stand on the beach and watch the
saloon burn.

INT. SHERIFF'S OFFICE - MORNING

Sheriff John Hicks Adams sits behind his desk drinking a cup
of coffee. He's reading the newspaper.

As he turns it over he sees a picture that makes him stop and
sit up.

He reads the title of the article and looks at a black and white picture.

The paper reads - "WILD MAN CAPTURED IN PORT ANGELES!"

He reads the caption of the photo. The caption reads - "SEEN ABOVE IS A GENT POSING WITH TURNOW. TO THE REAR IS JACOB MILLER, THE MAN WHO BROUGHT THE WILD MAN DOWN."

It shows a corpse in a casket with two men beside it.

One man is smiling, posing, the other is half turned but looking straight at the camera.

He looks at it for a long moment. Bert comes rushing in.

He looks at the Sheriff and looks at the paper.

> BERT
> It's him, Sheriff. He's using your
> wife's maiden name. What are you
> going to do?

The Sheriff looks out the window. Without turning to look at Bert, he speaks.

> SHERIFF
> Go down and get two tickets for the
> steamship out to Olympia. We leave
> tomorrow.

INT. BILL'S CABIN - NIGHT

Han wakes to find himself tied to a chair and gagged. Bill is in front of him with his back turned to him.

Han is in the small living room and Bill is poking at a fire in a potbelly wood stove.

He pulls out the red hot glowing end and holds it up to Han's face.

Han tries to scream and struggle, but he can't move and his cries are muffled in the gag.

Bill pulls the gag out of his mouth slowly. Han is crying.

> HAN
> Please! What do you want? Please,
> I'll give you all the money I have,
> please.

                    BILL
          You know why you're here. You were
          just here the other day, remember?

                    HAN
          Please, I'll give you money. Gold
          coins.

                    BILL
          You think I want your filthy money?

Bill shoves the poker into Han's boot. It sizzles and smokes
and Han cries in fear.

                    HAN
          Please! No! Please!

                    BILL
          Those boots won't last long. Then
          it's tender yellow flesh.

The boot burns through and the poker burns Han's foot with a
sick sizzling and popping sound.

Han howls in pain. Tears run down his cheeks.

Bill turns and puts the poker back in the fire.

                    BILL
          Why? Why did you kill her? She was
          your own daughter for Christ's
          sake.

                    HAN
          Please! I have many gold coins,
          please don't kill me!

                    BILL
          Tell me why!

He turns and puts the freshly heated poker into Han's other
boot.

Han howls again. Bill presses and the poker burns through his
foot and sticks into the floor, a sickly, greasy smoke rising
from it.

Han whimpers. Bill looks at him and grabs his head, turning
it roughly so that Han's ear faces his mouth.

He whispers into Han's ear.

                    BILL
          I loved her, you slant-eyed yellow
          devil. Now, I'm going to watch as
          you burn in hell.

                    HAN
          I killed her because she was a
          whore! Because you made her a
          filthy whore! She was mine, not
          yours! She was mine! She was mine!

Bill grabs another poker stick and spreads burning logs from
the wood stove onto the rough timber floor.

Han screams.

                    HAN
          She was mine! You had no right! No!
          AHHH!

Soon the cabin is ablaze. Bill goes to the bedroom and folds
a blanket over Ling's body.

He lays a wooden cross on top of her. He leaves the cabin as
it becomes engulfed.

Bill stands outside and watches it burn.

EXT. PORT ANGELES - MORNING

A group of people are stand outside of the Olympian House.
It smolders from a gaping black hole in the rear left side.

Jacob, Tracy, and Frankie stand in the rubble near the back,
looking over the horrible scene in the early morning light.

The office was the center of an explosion and the safe is
destroyed.

All the contents are gone or scattered and burnt. Frankie is
looking around sullenly.

Tracy approaches Frankie, whose face is covered in blood and
fire soot

Tracy pulls out a large stone wrapped in a skin. She holds it
out.

Frankie's eyes grow large and a dirty hand reaches out and
snatches it up.

She reaches out and slaps Tracy hard on the face. She looks
back at the smoldering wreckage, to the stone, then to Tracy.

FRANKIE
You! I thought it was that crook
Buster Kelly! You did this?

TRACY
No, Frankie, I swear. I...

FRANKIE
You what?

TRACY
I went to get this.

Tracy holds out a small pistol and Frankie looks at it.

TRACY
When I grabbed it, I heard a
commotion and saw the man with the
torch. I knew how valuable this was
to you... so I grabbed it. I don't
exactly know why, something just
told me it was the right thing to
do. Please, Frankie, you have to
believe me. Why else would I give
it back?

Jacob comes over and watches, but says nothing. Frankie still
stares at Tracy. Then, she sighs and relaxes.

She reaches out and hugs Tracy. Surprised, Tracy slowly hugs
her back.

FRANKIE
Thank you, Tracy, thank you. I'm
sorry I'm so hard on you. I just
expect more from you sometimes. But
you did good. I won't forget it.

Tracy smiles and they hold each other. Frankie looks at
Jacob.

FRANKIE
And thank you. You saved my life. I
won't forget that, either.

Jacob nods grimly.

JACOB
Now, if you ladies will excuse me,
I have some business to attend to.

Jacob leaves them holding each other.

106.

EXT. WOODS - DAY

Siya and Chuk-wa-tal walk along an old, narrow path in the
ancient, moss covered woods.

They come to a place where the path overlooks a small river
that runs swiftly through the woods.

They sit and Siya takes some dried fish from a pouch he has
hanging from his side.

He gives some to Chuk-wa-tal and they drink from a water
skin.

                    SIYA
          What did you think of the tribe's
          victory over the Cowichan? How did
          that make you feel?

                    CHUK-WA-TAL
          It made me scared, Siya. I think it
          was unwise to use guns, and even
          worse to deceive the people like
          that.

Siya looks at him and nods slowly.

                    SIYA
          But, why are you scared?

                    CHUK-WA-TAL
          Well, I think that it is asking for
          trouble to get so bold in taking
          matters like this into our own
          hands. The white men already want
          to move us to the reservation. If
          we grow too bold they will
          eventually find an excuse. That
          will be bad for all the people.

Siya nods and smiles.

                    SIYA
          Good, very good. You see with good
          eyes, my son. You will be a great
          leader one day, I think. Much
          better than Tik-wo-tan or Sik-way.
          I too fear that their way will be
          the way of sure and swift
          destruction for the people.

                    CHUK-WA-TAL
          So, we are going to the healing
          waters to ask for guidance for the
          people?

                    SIYA
          We are going because we need
          guidance. And our people will soon
          need a new leader.

                    CHUK-WA-TAL
          But, I'm not a leader Siya. I just
          want to see the people prosper and
          stay in our home.

                    SIYA
          That's why they need you. Come, we
          have a long journey still.

They get up and continue up the trail.

INT. SLOOP - DAY

Kelly, Gundersen, and Pete sit at a small table in the cabin
of the sloop.

They are counting a stack of bills and coins. Kelly smokes a
cigar. He slams his fist on the table sending coins flying.

                    KELLY
          Where's the stones, dammit? We risk
          all for this small pile of change,
          and no god damn stones! I trusted
          you fools!

                    GUNDERSEN
          She must have moved them. Maybe she
          was wise to us.

                    PETE
          Maybe you told her we was coming?

                    GUNDERSEN
          You calling me a turncoat? Maybe
          you was in it with her and made
          yourself a sweet little deal?

                    KELLY
          You fools, shut it! You're both too
          stupid to double-cross me, I know
          that much. She must have them
          hidden somewhere else.

                    PETE
          The cowboy saved the bitch's life.
          She would have died in the fire.
          She ran in after we blew the safe
          and I brained her and left her to
          burn. Maybe she gave them to him to
          protect.

                    KELLY
          We're going to have to do something
          about our old friend once and for
          all. And I know just what to do.
          We're going to set a little trap
          for our interfering friend.

EXT. TSE-WHIT-ZEN VILLAGE - DAY

Lt. Merryman and a group of soldiers approaches the longhouse
on horse back.

People stream out of the buildings and gather around them.

Merryman dismounts his horse and so do his men. They all are
armed.

Merryman pulls a paper from a pocket and begins to read
loudly.

                    MERRYMAN
          Attention! I'm Lt. Merryman of the
          United States Navy, acting agent of
          Indian Affairs for the Territory of
          Washington of the United States of
          America. I have a federal warrant
          here today to detain twelve men in
          the murder of thirty four-men,
          women, and children. These men will
          surrender themselves without
          indecent or we will forcibly detain
          the whole village until the
          culprits are found.

A murmur rises through the crowd, and people start to talk
confusedly. Tik-wo-tan comes forward.

                    TIK-WO-TAN
          Who are these men you seek, and
          what proof do you have that they
          are guilty?

                    MERRYMAN
          We have an eyewitness account from
          a survivor, the lone survivor. And
          this.

He takes out a whale bone club.

                    MERRYMAN
          Which carries your tribe's
          inscription.

He hands the paper to Tik-wo-tan.

                    MERRYMAN
          Now, you will turn these men over
          or we will forcibly remove you all
          now. What will it be? Make your
          choice quickly.

Tik-wo-tan stands, defeated. He passes the paper back and
starts to point to men.

As he points, soldiers grab the men. They cry out and resist.

The men are rounded up and shackled. Lt. Merryman looks over
the list and then the men.

He comes back to Tik-wo-tan and points at a name on the list.

                    MERRYMAN
          This one. We need this one.

Tik-wo-tan looks at him for a moment, then points at Sik-way.
The soldiers grab him and he struggles, fighting.

A soldier clubs him with his rifle stock. As they drag him
away he points at Tik-wo-tan and cries out.

                    SIK-WAY
               (in English)
          Him buy guns! His guns! His plan!
          His plan!

Lt. Merryman watches this and then nods to a soldier standing
nearby. He grabs Tik-wo-tan.

                    TIK-WO-TAN
          Wait, no wait! You can't! Wait!

The soldier strikes him on the temple with his gun stock and
he crumples.

110.

They throw him on a horse and march the other men in front of
the horses.

Lt. Merryman looks over the confused people standing around.

                    MERRYMAN
          From now on, you better understand
          there is only one law now. If you
          take the law into your own hands,
          we will find you and you will pay
          the price. Follow the laws given to
          you and leave justice to those men
          given the authority to carry it out
          by law. These men are hereby
          sentenced to life in a hard labor
          camp. Let this be a caution to
          those who would be emboldened to
          tempt their own fate. There is only
          one law, and only one justice.

He looks them over again then turns and rides away.

INT. MARSHAL'S OFFICE - DAY

Marshal is sitting behind his desk reading a piece of paper.

Jacob comes in. He picks up the badge that says "Deputy" that
is lying on the Marshal's desk and pins it to his jacket.

Marshal stands.

                    MARSHAL
          Well, I see you've made your
          decision. God damn glad to have
          you, Jake.

He sticks his hand out for Jacob to shake. Jacob takes it and
smiles slightly and nods.

                    JACOB
          Marshal, I've got someone who can
          testify against Black Pete for the
          murder of those two men last week.
          He was also the one that set the
          fire and explosion last night at
          the Olympian House.

                    MARSHAL
          Well, now. Slow down, boy. Let's
          take one thing at a time. First,
          that's good news. A witness on
          Black Pete. Damn good news - if the
          witness you have is credible.
                    (MORE)

                    MARSHAL (CONT'D)
          No judge in the territory will hold
          up the testimony of a whore.

                    JACOB
          How about Madame Frankie herself?
          And half a dozen whores and the
          barman?

                    MARSHAL
          Well, now. That is a little
          different. You have all this
          firsthand from Frankie?

                    JACOB
          She and the rest saw him murder the
          two men in cold blood. And the
          fire, well, I was in the place when
          it burned. I pulled her from the
          flames. Pete brained her just
          before he fled and left her for
          dead.

                    MARSHAL
          I see. Well, in that case, I guess
          we have a man to go get. You wait a
          few and I'll come with you.

                    JACOB
          That's all right, Marshal. You sit
          tight. I can handle this one.

Jacob grabs a pair of manacles and turns to leave.

                    MARSHAL
          Jacob. Bring him back here alive.
          We are going to see him to trial,
          then to the gallows to watch him
          hang. That's how we do things here.
          There's only one way.

Jacob looks at him and nods. Then he leaves.

EXT. WOODS - SUNET

Siya and Chuk-wa-tal climb over a rocky point above a swift
river high on the mountainside.

They crest the hill and see steaming pools of water. They
climb down to them.

Chuk-wa-tal sees Siya look at him and he smiles. Siya nods
and starts to chant softly.

They enter the water and they dip in the water. They both
sing louder now, together.

Siya stops and puts his head down. He sits in the water.

Chuk-wa-tal sits next to him in the steaming pool.

> SIYA
> In the long ago, a man of our
> people knew this place. My
> grandfather told me the story of
> him long ago. I want to give it to
> you now.

Chuk-wa-tal smiles at him.

> CHUK-WA-TAL
> Thank you, Siya. But, why didn't
> you tell me before, after my
> journey?

Siya laughs a hearty laugh. He pats Chuk-wa-tal on the head.

> SIYA
> You are young still, my son. But,
> it is good to be young. I was
> awaiting the right time to give you
> this story, because to give it to
> you I have to give my own story to
> you as well.

Chuk-wa-tal looks confused.

> CHUK-WA-TAL
> Your story? What do you mean, Siya?

> SIYA
> I mean I will give you two stories
> this night which you will always
> carry with you. It will be part of
> your own medicine. Now, listen and
> watch the sky, and don't look at me
> until the story is finished.

Chuk-wa-tal stares at Siya and he returns his gaze lovingly.

Reluctantly, Chuk-wa-tal looks away and stares at the sky.

> SIYA
> In the long ago, this man went on a
> journey much as you did. He found
> this place as well.
> (MORE)

                    SIYA (CONT'D)
He was so weary after his journey
that he thought that he must surely
have died and that these waters
were the spirit pools of rebirth.
He felt sad to have died, he
thought, but was glad as well that
his long journey was finally over.
As he sat in the steaming water,
his spirit was lifted from his body
and his spirit traveled free,
without his body for many days and
nights. After he had seen all the
places he couldn't go when he was
flesh and blood and weak, the top
of the highest mountain, the bottom
of the ocean, he decided next he
would see the heavens and stars and
find their secrets. He flew up to
the stars and found his ancestors
and great spirits were in the
heavens and they told him he had to
go back and save his people. They
said the earth would shake soon and
the ocean would rise and swallow
the people up. They told him he was
not dead but that he had a great
medicine that led him to this
special place, and that they had
called him there. They sent him
back and told him he must warn his
people of the shaking and that he
would become a great leader after
he had saved them. He said he
didn't want to go back, but they
promised that if he did they would
lead him here when his time was
done and that then he would become
great, not only in the flesh but in
the heavens as well, taking a place
among his great ancestors. So, he
went back and he saved his people.
Many didn't believe him, but many
did. They were the only ones saved
when the water came up and
swallowed the longhouses and washed
them away into the sea. He became a
leader for a time. Then, others
took his place. Soon, he became an
old man. Now look, my son, into the
night sky and you will see his
spirit as it joins his ancestors in
the heavens, where he has so longed
to go back to all these years.

114.

Chuk-wa-tal starts to say something, but a light in the sky catches his eye.

It's a green and blue light like a soft wavy cloud and it grows and dances brilliantly across the night sky.

Chuk-wa-tal watches and a tear comes to his eyes. His crystal glows brightly.

                    CHUK-WA-TAL
          Siya, it's so beautiful... Siya?

Suddenly the lights go out and he looks around. He's all alone.

He gets up and spins around, frantic. He stops and looks up and sees one last wave of light twinkle then the sky is dark again.

                    CHUK-WA-TAL
          NOOO! Siya!!

EXT. SHACK - NIGHT

Jacob is in front of a small wooden shack with a lantern and his pistol drawn.

INT. SHACK - NIGHT

Jacob kicks the door in and enters. The room is empty. He looks under the bed, behind the door.

EXT. SHACK - NIGHT

Jacob walks around the back of the shack. He sees an outhouse and goes to it.

He kicks open the door and points his gun in.

Empty.

He walks around it and sees a small boardwalk to the beach.

EXT. BEACH - NIGHT

Jacob follows the boardwalk until he arrives at a small skiff anchored on the beach.

Thirty yards offshore is anchored a small sloop. He gets in the skiff and launches.

EXT. SLOOP - NIGHT

Jacob boards the sloop. He looks around and sees nothing.

INT. SLOOP - NIGHT

Jacob goes down into the berth and looks around. Empty beer
bottles and refuse liter the floor and table.

He searches and finds nothing. He sighs. He turns to leave
and he hears a click as the hatch is closed to the deck.

He rushes to it and tries it. Locked. He bangs and yells.

>   JACOB
>   Who's there? This is the law and
>   I've got a legal warrant for Black
>   Pete. Open or I'll blast my way
>   out!

He takes out his pistol and aims at the door. Then, he hears
something behind him.

He looks down and sees a black snake at his feet. He turns to
shoot it and feels a searing pain in his leg as the snake
strikes with lightning speed.

He cries out and shoots it. Another one drops from a
cupboard.

He falls to his knees and shoots again and again at the
second snake.

His eyes go blurry and he tries to shoot again but hears the
chamber click empty.

He sees a fuzzy boot in front of him before he goes black and
a voice seemingly far away laughing a familiar laugh.

A face with no nose comes into view right in front of his.

It smiles a grotesque smile.

>   PETE
>   Welcome to hell.

INT. SALOON - MORNING

Marshal walks into the damaged, but now cleaned saloon. He
sees Frankie behind the bar stocking bottles.

                    MARSHAL
          Frankie, have you seen my new
          deputy?

                    FRANKIE
          Deputy? You mean Jacob?

                    MARSHAL
          What, he didn't tell you? I thought
          you were his key witness. I
          deputized him the day before
          yesterday and he went to bring
          Black Pete in based on your
          testimony. He never came back. I
          rode out to Port Crescent because I
          thought maybe he rode out there for
          some reason, but no ones seen him.
          Or Kelly and Pete.

                    FRANKIE
          Well, we talked about Pete killin'
          those men and I said I'd be willin'
          to testify if only someone'd bring
          the bastard in. But, I haven't seen
          him since that mornin'. I haven't
          seen that bastard Kelly since the
          day before the fire.

                    MARSHAL
          Shit, I knew I shouldn't have let
          him go alone.

                    FRANKIE
          I'd say not.

They stare at each other for a moment. Then two men walk in:
the Sheriff and Bert.

They look around and walk up to Marshal and Frankie.

                    SHERIFF
          Good morning ma'am, Marshal. My
          name is Sheriff John Hicks Adams
          from San Jose County, California.
          I'm looking for my son, Jake Adams.
          You might know him as Jacob Miller.

Marshal and Frankie look at each other in disbelief.

EXT. SKID ROAD - DAY

A man leads a bull team down a skid road pulling a large load
of logs.

He is whipping the bulls and calling loudly as he does.

Suddenly he stops and sees a man with blood soaked clothes and hands, face covered in black soot and stalking through the woods beside the road.

He watches as he goes, turning to stare at him with dead eyes then turns and walk on, melting into the trees.

The man stares as he goes.

INT. SLOOP - DAY

Jacob is tied up in the hold of the sloop. He opens his eyes slowly.

His eyes are still blurry but start to clear. He is naked except for a pair of thin underpants.

He sees Pete, Kelly, and Gundersen in front of him. They throw a bucket of cold water over him.

He gasps and catches his breath. They slap his face several times.

Kelly kneels in front of him.

> KELLY
> Welcome back, Mr. Miller. You had a nasty little bite from our friend black mamba. You know that's how Black Pete here got his name don't you? It's his specialty, using a black mamba. Or did you think it was just because he is black? Luckily, we have big plans for you, so we gave you some anti-venom to bring you back to life. We just wanted you to feel death for a few tasty moments, before we woke you up to play some more. And don't think about rescue, or escape. We've been sailing for at least forty-eight hours now. We're well out of reach of any of your new friends. Your all ours now. And we have so much planned for you.

Jacob closes his eyes and fades off. Another bucket of cold water hits him. He gasps and blinks awake.

                    PETE
          Don't go to sleep yet, sweetheart.
          We are just getting started. I have
          many more friends to introduce you
          to. Let's start with this.

He reaches down and picks up a slimy eel from a bucket. He
holds it with gloved hands. He brings it slowly to Jacob's
chest and touches him with it.

Jacob jumps and howls with pain. They laugh and do it again.

Screams echo across the empty water.

ON-SCREN TEXT: "TO BE CONTINUED..."

                                        FADE TO BLACK.

ABOUT THE SCREENWRITER

Ryan A. Herring grew up in the isolated but picturesque small town of Homer, Alaska. Having always lived in rural areas, he very naturally developed a deep love for the outdoors. He enjoys hiking, fishing, snowboarding, mountain biking, or to just be out exploring the mountains, rivers, and beaches of the Olympic Peninsula.

The rugged beauty of the Pacific Northwest has always been his main source of inspiration as a storyteller, as well as the stranger than fiction tales from the past. With a keen interest in the late 19th century history of the Pacific Northwest in particular, he also has a deep respect and passion for Pacific Northwest Native American cultures.

He worked as a carpenter by trade before becoming an independent filmmaker and author. He lives in Port Angeles, Washington, in the heart of the Olympic Peninsula, with his beautiful wife and two children.